The Remaking of Corbin Wale

ROAN PARRISH

Edited by Julia Ganis

Cover design by Natasha Snow

Layout by L.C. Chase

Second edition, March, 2018

Copyright © 2017 by Roan Parrish

Published by Monster Press

MONSTER PRESS

About Our Charity

Ten percent of the proceeds of this title will be donated to the Russian LGBT Network.

About the Russian LGBT Network

The Russian LGBT Network is an interregional social movement that unites various LGBTQI(+) initiatives across Russia. In the headquarters in St. Petersburg a team of 15 activists work every day to promote human rights, to fight inequality in Russia, and to build a strong and powerful community of LGBTQI(+) activists and their allies.

The Network provides various services to the community: we offer psychological and legal assistance to the people in need. The Network also provides Emergency assistance to the LGBTQI(+) people, who suffer persecution and prosecution, who find themselves in dangerous situations and fear for their lives and wellbeing. They are also working to assist LGBT people in the Chechen Republic who are being persecuted, unlawfully detained, tortured and killed to flee the republic, to restore their feeling of safety and security, and to find sanctuary outside of Russia.

Their philosophy is that human right defenders and the civil society are capable of ending LGBTQI(+) inequality all over the world. We, the team of the Russian LGBT Network thank you for showing you solidarity with the cause. When we unite our efforts, we can create a better tomorrow.

If you would like to submit a separate donation, please click the donation button on their webpage lgbtnet.org/en.

For my sister. May we die on the same day.

Darkness cannot drive out darkness; only light can do that.
— Martin Luther King Jr.

Part One ❧ Earth

Alex

Chapter One

ALEX BARROW LIKED BRINGING things to life.

A month ago, he'd had friends, a lover, and a prestigious job in New York. A week after that, he'd found himself back in his Michigan hometown, where he hadn't spent more than a week since leaving a dozen years before. He had nothing to his name except—now—the bakery where he stood. And yet, alone in the predawn dark of opening day, Alex felt lighter than he had in years. He took a deep breath of leaf-scented air and felt himself grin. Yes, Alex liked bringing things to life, and he'd dragged this bakery into being from the wreckage of his life in New York.

It had begun with the one-two punch of Timo breaking up with him, and Rustica, the restaurant in the West Village where Alex had worked as pastry chef for four years, being bought by a corporate conglomerate. Down a boyfriend and a job in forty-eight hours, Alex hadn't been sure which had been the bigger blow. And that, his best friend Gareth had pointed out with a knowing wink, should tell him something important about both.

Timo was a radiologist who owned the apartment they'd lived in. He was mature, sensible, handsome, and intelligent. He'd had a three-year plan, a five-year plan, and a ten-year plan, all of which, he'd explained patiently during the conversation that turned into a highly civilized breakup, had included Alex. That Alex hadn't known he was included in these plans had been a problem. That he'd had very little interest in them, once he'd been told, had been a more telling problem.

As Alex had lain on the couch that night—because Timo was far too mature and measured to suggest he leave suddenly, but

Alex had found it too strange to share a bed with the man who had been his partner and suddenly wasn't—he'd realized he felt . . . not nearly as much as he'd expected. Certainly less than he'd imagined he should feel after being with someone for three years, living with them for two, meeting their family, sharing their bed, and knowing how they tasted and what made them cry.

And he'd thought maybe Timo felt less than he'd expected too.

Losing Timo had certainly been an inconvenience, in that it had left Alex without a place to live. Walking into Rustica the next night to the announcement of its sale, on the other hand, had been gutting. Finding out the following afternoon that he could keep his job if he simply produced the menu the corporate team designed, but would no longer have the freedom to develop his own recipes, had been devastating. With no apartment, he certainly needed the salary. But he didn't want to be a machine, turning out the same pastries week after week, year after year. That was why he'd left his first two jobs at traditional bakeries. With no creative control and no power over the menu, he'd been bored as paste.

He'd left Rustica and walked through Lower Manhattan for hours, making pro and con lists in his head. When his phone had buzzed with an incoming call from his mother, Alex had almost ignored it, not wanting to admit failure on two fronts to the woman who only ever wanted to see him happy. But he'd answered anyway, and listened to her chat about the weather, the latest football game that had backed up traffic all the way to her house, a new store that had opened across the street from Helen & Jerry's Java. As he listened, he'd calmed thinking about the Ann Arbor autumn.

About the way the days were warm but the nights turned cold as soon as the sun's heat had burned away. The way downtown smelled like coffee and waffle cones and turning leaves and moss. The way the U of M fight song blasted from car horns and house windows and cell phone ringtones during football season and got stuck in your head even if you weren't a football fan.

When his mom had told him that, lately, the arthritis in her hands had gotten so bad she could no longer even make the coffee drinks at Helen & Jerry's Java—the café she and his father had opened his senior year in high school, and which his mother had run alone since his father died ten years ago—and that she wished she could take a vacation, drive up north with her new beau (her term), Alex's head had gotten fuzzy. And then it had gotten very, very clear.

"Mom," he'd said softly. "I think I'm coming home."

And now here he was. He'd shipped his belongings, surprised but not upset to find that he didn't own much he cared enough to hold onto. He'd given Rustica his notice, and he'd booked a flight. When he'd touched down in Detroit, it hadn't felt like moving, it had felt like visiting, as he'd done dozens of times before.

He'd had one small duffel bag and his laptop, as if he were coming in for a long weekend like he always did. The taxi had dropped him off in his mother's driveway, just like it always did, and his mother had come out to meet him, just like she always did. She'd told him he looked so handsome, just like she always did, and he'd seen the moment her eyes moistened, thinking about how she wished his father were here, just like he always did.

It was just the same, only everything was different.

Because this time, when his mother settled him at the kitchen table with a cup of coffee and a cup of decaf for herself, she didn't say, "So, tell me everything," like she always did. This time she said, "So, here's the plan."

Now, after weeks of work, the bakery that had existed in his head for years, in gradually shifting menu concepts, color combinations, and layouts, was finally a reality. Helen & Jerry's Java was now And Son. Gareth had thought it was a ridiculous name; Alex's mother had cried.

Alex could say now—armed with knowledge of the restaurant industry and professional baking training—that Helen & Jerry's Java had not been a good coffee shop. The layout had been bad, the coffee mediocre, and the pastries . . . well, the less said about them the better. Alex had completely transformed it. His mother's employees had jumped at the chance to log extra hours painting, cleaning, rearranging, and running endless errands. It had been pure luck that Mira, one of the baristas who'd worked there for a few years, had announced that she'd worked construction for her father all throughout high school. Alex had paid her to build out the counter and add a bench along the perimeter of the café.

While they'd worked behind paper-taped windows, Alex had spent his time sourcing ingredients, setting up deliveries, and designing his menu.

The best bakeries had a cohesive vision. You didn't want a counter selling bran muffins next to key lime tarts next to baklava next to polvorones. The menu needed to have range, but not feel chaotic—provide surprises, but not overwhelm. For each recipe he added to the mental menu in his mind, Alex had shifted another one off. When he'd realized he needed a lemon glaze on this one or cayenne in that one, it sparked to life another avenue of flavors.

He'd felt like a kid, sitting cross-legged on the heavy steel prep table, scribbling his dream recipes on sticky notes that he rearranged over and over on the cool metal. He had so many things he wanted to try, so many ideas that he eventually stuck all the notes back into a stack, put them on the shelf, and said to himself, *Ten and five. Ten basics and five specials. Start there and you can add more later.*

Alex had always had a bit of a problem reining it in.

And Son was reopening on a crisp, cool Monday that smelled of rain that didn't fall. Alex had been there since 3:30 that morning, baking, and when his employees showed up at 6:30, he smiled at the sounds of surprise they made as they looked around the finished bakery.

"It's amazing!" Mira called as Alex came out from the kitchen. Sean, the other barista who'd worked for his mom, agreed.

"Thanks to you," he said, and smiled at Mira. But he was really pleased with how it had turned out.

6

The walls of the seating area were sage green and behind the counter a warm terra cotta. Pen and ink drawings hung in untreated wood frames. Gone was the clutter of small tables and too many chairs. In their place were several four- and six-top tables, and a long padded bench with tables ran around the perimeter of the café under the windows.

There were plants in the corners, potted succulents on small wooden shelves on the walls, and air plants hanging from the pressed tin ceiling. The whole effect was calm and warm and peaceful.

The earthy bite of coffee, the comforting smell of fresh-baked bread, and the snap of sugar made Alex's stomach rumble, and he took a cinnamon streusel muffin back into the kitchen with him. He snapped a picture of himself taking a huge bite and sent it to Gareth.

Alex had met Gareth their first day of culinary school, and they had quickly become friends and then roommates. For ten years, Gareth had been the one constant in an otherwise hectic and chaotic life. Alex felt the ache of distance that he hadn't felt since the first year after his father died, when he'd wake up some mornings and remember all over again that he was gone. It had been Gareth he'd called from Ann Arbor when his mother sat him down a month before and told him she'd signed over the café to him. Gareth who'd told him he'd be an idiot if he didn't turn the café into a bakery of his own.

Happy opening day! Gareth wrote back in response to the muffin pic. *Try not to eat ALL the stock.* Then, a second later, *I'm proud of you.*

The warm feeling in Alex's stomach persisted as he slid a tray of croissants out of the oven and added notes to his recipe binder.

When they unlocked the door at seven, Alex's mother was the first to walk through. He hadn't let his mom see the bakery at all, and her mouth fell open as she looked around. She shook her head at him, and he saw the moisture in her eyes as she pulled him down for a fierce hug.

"I still think it should've been '& Son,' with an ampersand," she said, sniffing.

"Mom, I told you, it's harder to search for, and hard to put in a website URL. People don't know what it's called, so they'll say, 'It's called & Son, but with that and-sign thingy.' Besides, *And* is good for alphabetical listings, or—"

"Okay, okay, you know what you're doing and I should butt out, I hear you," she conceded, walking to the counter to greet Mira and Sean.

A man had trailed in after her and was standing politely off to the side. Alex turned to him and held out his hand. "You must be Lou Wright. I'm Alex. It's nice to meet you."

Lou grinned at him as they shook. He had mischievous brown eyes, dark brown skin, a bald spot, a warm smile, and an easy manner. Alex could see immediately why his mother liked him.

Alex got his mother and Lou coffee and croissants to go, and was about to retreat to the kitchen when someone approached the counter. Someone Alex couldn't look away from.

The man was a few inches shorter than Alex's six feet, and slim—almost willowy. He had a tangle of dark hair that fell around his face, and eyes almost as dark. His skin was light gold and there was a spray of freckles across his delicate nose. He looked up at Alex, eyes half hidden behind that veil of hair, with his head cocked like a bird.

"Coffee, please."

He was the most beautiful man Alex had ever seen. Strange looking, a bit awkward, and half-wild, the way animals were that lived side by side with people but never went inside as pets. His face and the set of his shoulders made Alex want to tramp through the woods as the leaves fell, run through fields to tumble him down on sun-warmed grass, press flowers to his lips to see which were softer. Beautiful.

"Hi," Alex said. "Hello. Good morning. Welcome to And Son. I just opened."

The man cocked his head in the other direction and nodded.

"Coffee," he said quietly. His tone said it was a request even though his voice didn't go up at the end to intone the question.

"Of course." *Get a grip, Alex.* "Light, medium, or dark roast?"

He shrugged one shoulder. "Dark." His voice was low and soft, and there was something so familiar about him all of a sudden that Alex narrowed his eyes against the jolt of déjà vu. But that's how it was coming back to Ann Arbor. Always the sense of familiarity paired with that jarring discontinuity.

Under Alex's scrutiny, the man dropped his chin a little and glared.

"Coming right up," Alex said. "Can I get you anything to eat?"

The man shook his head, but the glare was gone, and as he handed over his money, it was replaced by a faraway look that made Alex feel like he wasn't seen any longer. He brushed the man's palm with his fingertips as he took the bills, and their eyes locked for a moment. Then the man jerked away.

He didn't put anything in his coffee, just cradled the mug as he made his way to the corner table and folded himself onto the bench, knees sharp through faded denim. He slid a black notebook out of his tattered canvas bag and immediately bent so close over it that the ends of his hair brushed the paper.

He seemed completely absorbed in whatever was in the book, and after a while Alex went back to the kitchen, leaving the front of house to Mira and Sean.

When Alex brought baguettes out to the counter at lunchtime, the man was still there. He was still hunched over his book, but now he was drawing, his lines fluid, quick, and studied.

"Do you know that guy?" Alex asked Mira.

"Corbin Wale," she said softly. "He's come in for years, according to Helen—er, your mom. Since before I started working here. Sometimes he's here every day for two weeks, sometimes once a week, sometimes he doesn't show for a month. He always sits and draws. Helen always let him." She bit her lip. "Is it okay? Or do you want me to . . ."

"No, it's fine. I was just curious. Thanks." Mira looked relieved.

Alex sliced a piece of warm baguette in half, spread one side liberally with salted butter, and scooped plum jam into a ramekin. He put it all on a plate and carried it over to the table in the corner. Corbin didn't look up. He didn't seem to notice Alex at all.

"Corbin?" he said softly.

Corbin jerked, his elbow nearly knocking the empty coffee cup off the table. The eyes that met Alex's were wide and wild.

"Sorry," Alex said. He kept his voice soft and smiled. "I thought maybe you might like a snack." He set the plate down on the table and took a step back, since Corbin seemed threatened by his looming.

"I didn't . . . I didn't order that." Corbin blinked quickly as if he was coming out of a dream, confused about what was real and what wasn't.

"No, I just thought you might like it." At the gaping mouth and fluttering eyelashes, he added, "Since I just reopened, I wanted to welcome customers. You used to come in when this was my mom's place, right?"

"Your mom. Helen is your mom."

"Yep. She asked me to take the place over. It's been a lot of work for her lately. She gets tired."

"Tired," Corbin echoed, and his shoulders slumped a bit, like the word had taken up residence in his body.

"I'm Alex. It is Corbin, right? That's what Mira said." He nodded at his employee and she smiled.

Corbin gave a stuttering nod. His eyes tracked from the food on the table to Alex's face. "You don't want me to leave." Alex realized that he said all his questions like statements.

"No. I'm glad you're here." It was a pat answer—one any new business owner would give a customer—but Alex felt the truth of it down to his toes. "Please make yourself at home."

Alex tried to get a glimpse of what Corbin was working on, but the notebook was covered by Corbin's arms, intentionally or not. All that was visible were some spiky black lines and an indigo curve arcing from under Corbin's fine-boned wrist.

"Well, I'll leave you to it," Alex said, and turned back to the kitchen. As he got out the flour and butter to make pie crust, he realized what he felt was a vague sense of disappointment. Disappointment that he hadn't seen the contents of the notebook. Disappointment that Corbin hadn't asked him to sit down and join him. Disappointment that Corbin had seemed to draw closer into himself with every inch toward him that Alex moved.

And when he brought two pies out later that afternoon, disappointment to find the table in the corner empty, with no sign of Corbin having been there at all.

Chapter Two

ALEX HAD A PROBLEM.

Alex had a problem and it was spelled C-O-R-B-I-N W-A-L-E.

The problem was that every morning Alex worked with bated breath, finding excuses to come out of the kitchen to see if Corbin was there. The problem was that when Corbin was there, Alex's eyes seemed magnetized to him—to the cant of his head on his graceful neck. To the way his thin, nail-bitten fingers wielded a pen like a scalpel, ruthless and exacting. To the hair that often obscured his face. To the eyes that either stared resolutely down, completely absorbed by his work, or fixed, dreamily, on something up and to the right that Alex didn't think he was seeing at all.

Alex would wait, hoping that some loud noise or sudden shift in the air would catch Corbin's attention. Snap him out of absorption or dream, and bring him back to a place where Alex could reach him.

It wasn't that Alex didn't try. Sometimes he even succeeded, for a little while.

The next time Corbin came in, Alex asked what he was drawing. Corbin looked up, startled, as if he hadn't realized his notebook was visible to anyone but himself. He looked at the page and then back at Alex, dark eyes framed in inky lashes.

"Everything," he said, and a shiver ran up Alex's spine.

A few days later, Corbin seemed out of sorts. Alex was working the cash register and when he asked Corbin how his day was going, Corbin muttered, "You can't talk to me today. Please."

"All right," Alex said. "I'm sorry."

Corbin's brows drew together, a line between them. "No, no."

Alex handed over his coffee without another word, and Corbin's hand trembled as he took it. He pushed crumpled-up bills onto the counter and slunk to his table in the corner, tangle of hair hiding his face completely. Alex watched as Corbin stared into space, worrying his bottom lip between his teeth in a manner that absolutely did *not* send a shock of tender desire through him.

Alex watched Corbin. His cup emptied, though Alex never saw him sip it, and rather than becoming absorbed in his notebook, he pulled his jacket tightly around himself and left as suddenly as he'd come.

He didn't come back for three days.

"HEY," Alex said when Corbin next came in. "I realized why you looked familiar. I think we went to high school together."

It had struck Alex as he was lying in his childhood bedroom one night, exhausted and wanting nothing but to fall into a dreamless sleep.

He'd closed his eyes on the day and instead of the grown-up Corbin, he saw a boy. Painfully skinny, with a messily shaved head like he'd run an electric razor over it himself. He had huge dark eyes and long lashes and his clothes were brown and green and gray, the colors of the forest, as if to announce the place he was camouflaged to fit in.

The boy had been a freshman when Alex was a senior, and he'd never known his name. It was a big school. Alex likely wouldn't have remembered him at all, except that a month or two into the school year, someone had spray painted *FOREST FAGGOT FREAK* on a bank of lockers outside the auditorium. The boy standing in front of the locker that was clearly the epicenter was this pretty, skinny boy, staring at the words like they had no meaning.

After that, the rumors about him had reached even the senior class. That he was gay. That he didn't deny it, and responded to neither taunts nor camaraderie. That he lived in the forest and animals followed him to school. That he spoke to them, but not to anyone else. That something was wrong with him.

Even then, Alex might not have remembered him. Might have grouped him in the category that his seventeen-year-old brain had marked Braver Than Me, because it felt easier not to tell anyone that he, too, desired boys instead of girls. Because it felt like he had something to lose.

But then the boy—Corbin—had disappeared.

The rumors flew. He'd gone feral in the woods. He'd been having an affair with a rich businessman and fled the country with him. He'd killed himself. Someone at school had found out he was actually a vampire and he'd had to leave town.

But here was Corbin in front of him—clearly not dead, likely not a vampire, as it was a sunny day, and not feral . . . not completely, anyway.

"Do you remember me?" Alex asked.

Corbin bit his lip and nodded.

"Oh, did my mom tell you?" It seemed likely that his mother had asked every customer who looked about his age if they'd gone to high school with her son.

Corbin shook his head. "I recognized you. You were a football player."

He supposed that had been the most notable thing about him to a stranger in high school, but for some reason it still made his stomach feel a little hollow to hear it.

Coffee in hand, Corbin nodded at him and went to sit down. While Alex worked, he scoured his mind for other scraps of memory about Corbin from high school. He found only one.

Alex had gotten to school late one morning and had to park at the farthest edge of the lot. He'd cut around the back of the school to the science wing, and had seen someone coming out of the tree line. A skinny boy, all large eyes, and hands and feet too big for his body. A dog had been trailing behind him. At the edge of the woods, he'd paused and spoken to the dog. Then he'd scratched its head, knelt, and thrown his arms around its neck. The boy had hugged the dog like it was his only friend in the world, then snapped his fingers, and the dog had bounded back into the forest. Alex thought it must have been the last time he'd seen him until Corbin had shown up at And Son.

At lunchtime, Alex cut a thick slice of the oatmeal bread he'd baked that morning and toasted it. He spread the hot toast with butter and sprinkled it with cinnamon and sugar. Corbin was bent over his notebook, drawing as usual, but this time when Alex approached, he pushed his hair out of his face and looked up. His eyes were huge.

"I brought you a snack."

He laid the plate on the table and hovered for a moment.

"That . . ." Corbin pointed at the toast suspiciously. "That's my favorite."

"Yeah?" Warmth flushed through Alex. Preparing food was always a pleasure, but this—preparing something for someone he liked and having them desire it—was the thrill of satisfaction. "I'm glad."

He couldn't help himself. He stayed in the hope that Corbin would eat it in front of him. When the man raised the toast to his full lips and took a bite, cinnamon and sugar spilling onto the plate like snow, something hot and possessive ripped through Alex.

Sugar stuck to Corbin's lips, and Alex wanted to bend over him and lick it from his mouth. Corbin's jaw clenched as he chewed, and Alex imagined Corbin on his knees before him, jaw moving for another reason entirely.

Corbin's throat worked as he swallowed, and Alex fisted his hands in front of him and turned quickly away.

"Okay, enjoy," he called over his shoulder, voice scraped raw with arousal and confusion.

He'd never responded to someone the way he responded to Corbin. He'd had lovers, he'd had good sex, he'd seen men across a room or over a pool table and felt attraction, lust.

With Timo, he'd felt desire, affection, love—or so he'd thought.

But Corbin had awoken something in him that felt like all of these, and none of them.

It was the difference between strawberry jam and a perfect, sun-ripe strawberry. Other people he'd desired had been jam. He'd seen them, liked them, saw potential in them, thought of what he might do with them, how they'd combine.

Corbin was a strawberry. If you had any sense at all, you took it as it was and you never questioned it. You didn't add sugar and you didn't add heat. You didn't put it in a sandwich or use it in a cake. You didn't do anything to it because it was already as absolutely, perfectly a strawberry as it would ever be. You recognized it, and were grateful for it.

And, if you were lucky, you savored it.

That was what Alex was doing.

Alex was savoring.

Chapter Three

THE FIRST TUESDAY IN NOVEMBER, it stormed. It began at noon with a clap of thunder and a silence just long enough for the patrons of And Son to freeze in anticipation, and then turn to each other and smile their relief that it was only thunder and no rain.

And then the rain came down.

Outside was black; rain hit the pavement and the roof like it was throwing itself down from the sky. The wind snatched it out of the air and lashed the windows with it. Umbrellas were torn from hands and plastic trash cans blew down the sidewalk like tumbleweeds. It only took thirty seconds for everything outside to be drenched.

Thirty minutes after that, it was still coming down, and the shop had emptied, customers running for their cars or trudging out, resigned to a soaking.

Except for one.

Corbin Wale sat in his corner and watched the rain.

He sat there for hours.

The weather app on Alex's phone said the downpour would result in flash flooding and continue all night. It was only four, but it seemed unlikely they'd get any more customers that afternoon, so he told his employees to clean up and go home.

As they cleaned out the display and zeroed out the cash register, Corbin watched the rain.

As they mopped the floor and wiped the tables, Corbin watched the rain.

As Mira, Sean, and Sarah left—wind blowing a spray of rainwater and wet leaves onto the freshly cleaned floor—and Alex locked the door behind them, Corbin watched the rain.

And Son glowed like a lighthouse in the rain-swept dark, and Alex approached him slowly. He lifted the chair across from Corbin and moved it back far enough that he could sit down.

Corbin's eyes were fixed on the rain as if he saw something in it he couldn't miss a moment of. Suddenly Alex wanted so badly to see what Corbin saw that the desire hit him like a physical pain.

He wanted to rest his hand on Corbin's and feel his skin, lace their fingers together and sit close as the rain whipped around them. He wanted to lift Corbin's hand to his lips and press a kiss to his knuckles. He thought Corbin would smell like ink and paper, coffee, and whatever the smell of Corbin was, just Corbin, beneath all the rest.

He wanted to push the man's hair back and cup his cheek. Trace the lines of his face with the pad of one finger, feather over dark brows and ruffle ink-black lashes.

He wanted to press his thumb into the dip in Corbin's lush lower lip, feel the flesh give like a ripe peach, push his fingers inside and feel the sharp edges of teeth and the rasp of tongue.

He wanted, wanted, wanted, like he had never wanted before.

But more than any of that, he wanted Corbin to talk to him. He wanted to be included in the cocoon of him, invited into Corbin's world.

In the glow of the bakery, with the hum of the coffee machine and the buzz of chatter stripped away, the only sounds were rain and wind outside.

Suddenly, Corbin's gaze snapped to him, though he'd been sitting there for at least a minute. Alex's breath caught. Corbin looked right at him, as present and clear as anyone.

"Did you know there's a phenomenon called phantom rain, where it's so hot that the raindrops evaporate before they hit the ground," Corbin said.

It was so unexpectedly . . . ordinary that Alex almost laughed. "No, I didn't."

"Everyone's gone." Corbin looked around like he'd just noticed.

"Yeah. I don't think anyone else'll be in when it's coming down like this."

"I should leave so you can go home."

Corbin began gathering up his notebook and pens, and Alex grasped around for a way to make the moment last.

"Do you want to help me make something?" Alex asked. "If you have time."

Corbin cocked his head, dark eyes curious. "In the kitchen." He said *kitchen* like it was an improbability.

Alex nodded and watched indecision flicker over his face, then curiosity, then Corbin dropped his chin so Alex couldn't see his face at all, and Alex's stomach lurched.

He reminded himself that he didn't know anything about Corbin, that they weren't friends yet, no matter how much he might wish they were.

Gareth had told him more than once that he exerted influence over people even when he didn't mean to. When Alex had asked him to explain, Gareth had shrugged and said that he couldn't explain why it was true. Just that when Alex had a plan, the plan came into being, and other people got caught up in it, from where to get dinner to where to go on vacation.

"You don't have to," he offered now.

But Corbin said, "Okay," and gathered up his things, slung the canvas bag over his shoulder, and stood up.

When Alex stood, he was just a few inches taller than Corbin, and closer to him than he'd ever been before. He shoved his hands in his pockets to keep from steering Corbin into the kitchen with a hand on the small of his back.

"What are we making," Corbin asked, dropping his bag beside the steel prep table.

"We're going to make brioche for tomorrow. It's better if you let the dough sit overnight." At Corbin's narrowed eyes, he added, "It's a rich buttery bread. I think it'll be nice for tomorrow. The day after bad weather, people like comforting things."

"Bread is comforting," Corbin said.

Alex couldn't tell if he was asking or agreeing, so he said, "I think it is."

"My aunts always made our bread."

"Is that who you grew up with?"

Corbin nodded and his eyes got that dreamy cast. "Bake on Saturday," he said, as if he was repeating part of a poem. Then his eyes refocused. "But it wasn't usually Saturday, I don't think."

"Did you bake with them?" Alex waved Corbin over and handed him the eggs and sugar to add to the mixer, where the yeast and water had dissolved.

"No." Corbin dumped in the sugar and watched as the water wetted it, like a lake eating into an island. Then he picked up an egg and stared at it.

After he'd looked at it for a minute, Corbin deftly cracked it against the lip of the bowl and added it to the mixer, then the others. When Alex closed the distance between them to flick the mixer on, he could feel the heat of Corbin's body next to his; the air between them felt supercharged. Corbin was watching the mixer the way he'd watched the rain, as if hypnotized.

But when Alex's shoulder pressed into his, Corbin jumped back a step, pulling his shoulders in, eyes gone wide.

Alex had a bad feeling in the pit of his stomach. He gritted his teeth at the thought that someone had hurt Corbin.

"Sorry." Alex and Corbin said it at the same time.

Alex shook his head. "Do you want to add the salt and flour?"

In they went, and the mixer began to turn again.

"I used to do this all by hand," Alex said. "In cooking school we had to learn all the techniques. Honestly, though, I love the mixer."

Corbin hummed in reply, but his whole attention was on the bowl. Alex's was on Corbin's face. His brows drew together with concentration, and his lashes threw shadows on his cheeks. He'd tucked his hair behind his ear so he could see. His ears were small and delicate, with a slight point at the top, and they stuck out a little, which Alex found adorable. He was also startled by how familiar they were. In high school, when Corbin's hair had been shaved, those ears had made people call him *fairy*.

Corbin pointed at the bowl and turned wide, excited eyes on Alex. The dough had finally come together.

Alex grinned. "Yeah, there's the moment when things are separate, and the moment when they're one thing, and you have to watch the whole time to see that instant when one becomes the other."

Corbin's smile was dangerous. It was slow and warm as fresh-baked bread, and then you saw teeth. A little crooked, charmingly overlapping in the front. The best smile Alex had ever seen. He was nervous what he might do to elicit another smile like that.

He could hardly tear his eyes away to swap in the dough hook. "Now the butter. One chunk at a time until it's incorporated."

Corbin did as he was told, watching intently.

"Hey, Corbin?"

"Hmm."

"What do you draw? I know, everything, but will you tell me about it?"

No answer as the butter turned the dough glossy, glossier. Alex scraped down the sides of the mixer and they watched as it came together. He turned off the mixer and covered the bowl, set it aside.

"I could show you," Corbin said softly.

"Please."

The notebook had a plain black cover and a flexible spine, and Corbin cracked it open, pages splayed out on the table. His finger-tips hovered over the paper like he was feeling as much as seeing. Or maybe hiding. With a deep breath, he nudged the book slightly toward Alex.

"I started drawing them ages ago," he said. "They were just

there one day. And I . . ." Corbin bit his thumbnail and blinked. Alex smiled as warmly as he could, wanting so much to hear.

Corbin flipped a few pages back. "I would draw stories for us. Adventures. Like we were hanging out. Because they were my friends, and I could take them with me like this. People at school didn't want to be my friends."

The sketchbook pages looked like a graphic novel. Alex recognized Corbin right away. He'd exaggerated everything about himself—the waves of his hair more tangled, his dreamy eyes glassy, his angles sharp enough to cut—and somehow it captured him perfectly, as if exaggeration exposed a truth of him that realism never could.

Also on the page was a woman who looked like a female version of Corbin, with her pointed elbows, feather-black hair, and matching oversized canvas jacket. But where Corbin's eyes were dreamy, hers were shrewd, and where Corbin was slender, her angles were packed with coiled muscle. She looked like she could take on anyone.

There was a tall black woman with short curly pink hair, dressed all in black and drawn only in profile. She had a hand resting on the head of shaggy gray dog—no, a wolf. The wolf's expression wasn't fierce, though, but docile and curious.

There was a small impish girl with pale skin and platinum hair, who seemed always to be in motion. She was plucking at one person's sleeve, or sneaking up on another. Her smile was sly.

Last was a large man with light brown skin and dark brown hair. He wore painter pants and a navy and white striped T-shirt, which made him seem to Alex like some kind of French sailor he'd seen in an old movie. The man was muscular and striking, and something about the detail in his renderings whispered to Alex that he was different from the others.

"Does it just sit there."

"What?" Alex glanced up from the sketchbook. "Oh. Yeah, it should rest for another hour, hour and a half. Guess it wasn't the most interesting thing I could've let you make."

Corbin cocked his head in confusion, and Alex remembered how absorbed he'd been. *Strike that.*

"Do you want to make something else while it's resting? What do you like? If I have the ingredients for it here, we can make it."

Corbin nodded. "Let me think." Then he went back to studying his sketchbook, and Alex smiled at the idea that he was going to actually stand there and think about it.

"Do they have names?"

"Of course. But I can't tell you."

"Oh. Why not?"

"Because names give you power over things. And only I get to have power over them."

Heat flushed through Alex at the intensity in Corbin's voice. He imagined what it would feel like to have Corbin writhing beneath him, calling his name. He thought that maybe the power of names went both ways.

He turned a few pages of the sketchbook, and saw a garden, then a house. It was a turn-of-the-century house, like those on the old west side of town. The roof slumped, the eaves sagged, and the windows gaped like broken teeth.

But the trees around the house were myriad lush greens and the wide back porch was inviting. One window glowed lighter than the others, and Alex imagined it was Corbin's bedroom.

"Is that your house?"

"It's my aunts' house."

"Do you live with them?"

"No. Not anymore. They're gone."

"I'm sorry. But you live here?"

"Yes. The Catsle."

"Castle?"

"No. Catsle. Aunt Hilda liked cats."

Alex flipped another page, then another. Corbin seemed to draw in real time, because the figures on the pages began wearing scarves and sweaters; the leaves on the trees around the Catsle began to change. Alex's fingers closed around the corner of the page and lifted it slowly, still taking in every detail on the page before him, and in the time it took him to turn it, Corbin moved.

He grabbed the sketchbook, closed it, and pulled it to his chest, crossing his arms around it.

"Um, cookies," he said. "A thing I like." His expression was a little panicked, but Alex thought he saw a slight flush to his cheeks. *What the hell was on the next page?*

"Okay, cookies it is."

Corbin slid the sketchbook back in his bag, pausing for a moment as if he was saying goodbye.

Alex pulled ingredients from around the kitchen. He remembered Corbin's face when he'd brought out cinnamon toast and smiled. "I bet you'd like snickerdoodles."

"Is that real." Corbin looked like a bird puzzled by why he couldn't fly through a windowpane.

"Yes." Alex grinned. "They're basically the cookie version of cinnamon toast."

Corbin's eyes got wide, then dreamy. "Mmm."

Alex had certainly used baking as seduction before. There was an intense sensuality to working with food. Moving around each other in the kitchen, touching and smelling the ingredients, tasting the food—it often led to touching, smelling, and tasting each other.

He could imagine how it might go. A hand on Corbin's shoulder as he leaned in to look at the mixture. The press of his chest against Corbin's back as he demonstrated how large to make the cookies. The feel of Corbin's tongue on his fingers as he fed him a bit of dough. The give of Corbin's lips when he replaced the dough with his mouth. They'd kiss until they were panting, then he'd spread Corbin out on the table and make a feast of him.

The cookies could burn for all he cared.

Alex shook his head and pinched the inside of his wrist to get his mind back together. It was clear that wasn't going to happen here, no matter how much he might want it to.

Rumors from high school aside, he had no idea if Corbin was

attracted to men. And even if he were, the few times Alex had touched him by accident—the brush of their hands as Corbin paid for his coffee, the press of shoulders as they stood—Corbin had jerked away like he'd been burned.

Besides, Alex didn't simply want to sleep with Corbin. He wanted Corbin to come back. To *keep* coming back. He wanted Corbin to ruffle aside his barriers, hold out a hand to Alex, and let him in.

So he talked about cookies. He talked about culinary school. He found out that Corbin grew vegetables and herbs in the garden behind his house, but cooked mostly simple things and sometimes forgot entirely. He learned that Corbin loved spices— cinnamon, ginger, nutmeg, all the warm flavors of autumn and winter—but didn't care for chocolate. He learned that Corbin had a lot of dogs.

"They hang around the yard and like to walk with me, but they're not exactly mine," Corbin explained. "Only one comes inside with me. Stick."

"The dog's name is Stick?"

"It's not really her name, just what I call her. Because she really likes when I throw sticks."

Alex smiled. *Names give you power over things.*

This dough they mixed by hand, and Alex felt a familiar calm settle over him.

"What's cream of tartar."

"It's an acid that's used as a leavener. When it's combined with baking soda, they produce carbon dioxide gas, which is the same thing that yeast in bread produces. It'll make the cookies soft."

"What else." *Okay, not bored by minutiae, then.*

"Well, it stabilizes egg whites when you whip them because it strengthens the bubbles so they don't deflate as fast. Um, you can add it to simple syrup and it'll magically stop it from crystallizing."

"Magically." Corbin's eyes narrowed, his gaze suddenly sharp.

"Well, no. Chemically. When the sugar is dissolved, the acid prevents it from re-bonding and forming crystals."

Corbin was watching him, dreamy again, and Alex found himself swallowed up in his dark eyes.

"It, uh. It's the residue left on the barrels after wine is fermented."

"Wow." Corbin smiled that slow smile again and Alex blundered over to turn on the oven before he did anything ill-advised.

"Okay, now we roll them into balls and coat them in cinnamon and sugar."

Corbin leaned in to sniff at the cinnamon and sugar mixture and immediately whipped away and sneezed five times in quick succession. He shook his head between sneezes like a cat, and Alex tried not to laugh. Then he got lost in the shift of muscle in Corbin's lithe forearms as he rolled his cookies in cinnamon and sugar.

After a few minutes, the smell of the baking snickerdoodles filled the kitchen.

"Smells like a rainy morning," Corbin said.

"Is that when you make cinnamon toast?"

One nod, and a faraway look.

"Did your aunts used to make it when you were little?"

"Yes. Aunt Jade made it on rainy mornings and when I couldn't sleep."

"How did you end up living with them?"

"I always lived with them. Since I was a baby."

"Your parents weren't around?"

Corbin shook his head. "No. When I was really young, my mom came by sometimes, when she was passing through town. She'd stay for a cup of coffee. My aunts said she drifted. Then she didn't come any more. My father died before I was born."

Thunder cracked loudly outside, and the kitchen went black.

"Oh no," Corbin murmured, and Alex instinctively moved toward the sound of him stumbling into something.

"Are you scared of the dark?" Alex reached for what he

thought was Corbin's shoulder, but his hand landed in Corbin's hair instead. The strands curved around his fingers like feathers.

"No." Corbin stepped just out of reach.

They stood in silence for a minute as their eyes adjusted, shapes resolving into familiar objects.

"Be careful of the oven," Alex said. He maneuvered around Corbin, who clearly didn't want to be touched, and opened the oven door, sliding the trays of snickerdoodles onto the counter. "We should let them cool for a few minutes. The way the cream of tartar keeps them soft also means they fall apart if you try and take them off the tray right away."

Alex could feel Corbin draw closer. His skin felt like it had been turned into a Corbin-seeking instrument, attuned to the other man's presence. Alex kept talking and Corbin drew closer. He talked about cookies. He talked about cinnamon. He talked about how opening this bakery was a dream he'd had for a long time, but hadn't believed he'd ever make a reality.

"Your mom gave you the coffee shop to open a bakery," Corbin said, in his strange intonation.

"She signed the coffee shop over to me, but she didn't tell me what to do with it. I don't think she cared, really, as long as it got me to stay in town, and she got to spend more time with her boyfriend."

"She must care about it. It's what she and your father built together."

"She told you that?"

"Everyone knows that," Corbin dismissed, but Alex wondered what else he knew.

"You've been coming here a long time, huh?"

"For a while."

"Why? It wasn't a very good coffee shop."

"Your mom was kind to me. She let me sit and didn't bother me. She didn't let other people bother me. I don't care about the coffee."

"Why do they bother you?"

Alex's eyes had adjusted to the dark enough that he saw Corbin's chin drop, saw him glance up through his hair and bite his lip. Saw his eyes flutter shut as he said, "Because. I'm a freak. I mess up everything I touch and people know it. They always have."

Alex's mouth crowded with denials, reassurances, and threats, but Corbin had spoken in a way that rendered them all useless. What came out of his mouth instead was, "I don't think you're a freak. I think you're great." And he handed Corbin a cookie.

Corbin held the cookie for a moment, let it rest in his palm like he was weighing it against the truth of Alex's words. Then he took a bite and the smell of cinnamon grew stronger.

"This is the most delicious cookie I've ever had," Corbin said, and smiled slightly in the dark.

Chapter Four

A FEW DAYS after the storm, Alex was putting fresh croissants in the display case when a man burst through the door enthusiastically.

"Alexander Barrow! I'm Mac—Barry MacKenzie, but everyone calls me Mac. Good to meet you."

He stuck out a hand and Alex shook it, though he had specific opinions about people who said that everyone called them anything.

Mac was forty-five or so, burly, and a bit on the short side. He was dressed in Michigan gear from head to toe.

"It's Alex. And nice to meet you, too. Can I get you something?"

"Oh, no, no, thanks. I brought you everything you'll need." He brandished a shiny blue U of M folder full of papers at Alex. "I'm the chairman of the Small Business Owners' Guild, but I'm sure your mom's told you all about it."

"Nope," Alex said, and Mac's face fell.

"Well," he said, recovering quickly, "no problem. All the info's in the folder. I own the Maize Cave."

Alex nodded. That made the Michigan apparel slightly more understandable, if no less ill-advised.

"Basically the SBOG works to keep all the business owners in town connected. This year, my initiative is to implement monthly theme days where all the biz owners will do something in their shops to reflect the theme. It works great on social media, so we figure it'll generate some buzz. Especially with the younger patrons, eh?" He squeezed Alex's shoulder, and Alex wanted to shake his hand off.

As Mac continued to monologue, Alex felt all the energy drain from him. This was one side of business ownership he didn't relish.

"Listen, thanks for the information, but I've got bread rising in the kitchen and I need to go check on it." He held out his hand.

A burst of laughter from one of the tables made them both turn. Mac's expression immediately soured, and he sneered. But it wasn't at the girls who'd laughed. It was at Corbin, ensconced in his customary place in the corner.

As if he felt eyes on him, Corbin looked up, and when he saw Mac, he froze. His pen dropped to the table. His wide eyes darted from Mac, who was still glaring, to Alex. Alex smiled at him the way he always did, but Corbin just blinked and gathered his pens and his notebook, shoving everything into his bag. Then he made his way to the door before Alex could say anything.

Mac shook his head as the door swung shut.

"Guess your mother asked you to let him loiter here."

"No. My mother doesn't make the decisions about who comes into my place of business. Besides, he's not loitering. He's a paying customer. A welcome customer."

Mac raised his palms as if to say Alex was overreacting, but he shook his head. "All right, but you be careful with that one. He's not the sort you want associated with your business, is all I'm saying."

"Oh? And why's that?"

Mac leaned in. "Kid's not right. Ask anyone."

"Okay, thanks for stopping by," Alex said, gritting his teeth and gesturing toward the door. As Mac left, Alex looked down the street, hoping Corbin was lingering nearby, but he was nowhere to be seen.

HE DIDN'T COME BACK until four days later.

"Hey," Alex said, stomach light and heart pounding. "I've missed you."

Corbin froze, then a slow smile crept across his lips and he blushed and looked down. "Hi."

When Alex brought him cinnamon toast around lunchtime, he smiled all over again.

FORTUNATELY, Mac seemed to be an outlier. Most of the other business owners Alex met were all right.

Meg Patterson ran Trek, an outdoors shop two doors down, and had known his mother for years. Dima and Luke Petrakis owned Hellas, a Greek diner on the corner. They'd fed him poutine made with feta cheese and parsley that he'd had dreams about. Caitlin and Doug Kleeman owned two fancy galleries down the street; Marsha Langhorn ran a bead gallery a block over; Andrea, Marge, and Lilly Kuehn owned the ice cream and chocolate shop that wafted deliciously when the wind blew.

Alex had dinner with his mom and Lou one evening, and learned that Lou's son, Orin, ran the Art Association two blocks from And Son. Alex remembered going there as a kid because they ran weekly art classes upstairs in the summertime. He remembered being ushered through the first floor gingerly so none of them would touch any of the art for sale.

Orin showed up a few minutes late for dinner, seeming a bit out of sorts, and apologized. Once the food came and they all talked for a while, though, he warmed up, and Alex thought he might see the promise of a friend. It would be nice to have one. Now that And Son was up and running, he had enough time to miss Gareth and his friends in New York.

Orin was about his age, or maybe a few years older. He had a low, soft voice and spoke as if he expected to be listened to. Orin looked nothing like his father. Where Lou was kind looking and a little goofy, Orin was intense and handsome. Where Lou's eyes were twinkly and mischievous, Orin's were piercing and gorgeous—the thickness of his long curling lashes almost giving the impression he wore eyeliner. His dark brown skin was flawless, almost luminous, and he had a widow's peak and close-cropped hair. Large, graceful hands and broad shoulders made him seem expansive, comfortable in his body. Despite his intensity, there was a sense of stillness about Orin that relaxed Alex.

During dinner, Alex found out that Orin hadn't grown up in Ann Arbor—he'd lived in Detroit with his mother—but had made his way here in his twenties when he and Lou had reconnected, and begun working at what was then a gallery space. He'd later become manager, and had bought it a few years ago when the previous owners retired. He'd left the downstairs space as a gallery and turned the upstairs of the building, where Alex had attended those long-ago classes, into a permanent space for programming. They ran family classes on Saturdays, drop-in classes on Sundays, after school classes during the school year. They'd just added a series of pay-what-you-can classes for veterans and a weekly free class for homeless residents.

"Orin's a potter," Lou said proudly, elbowing his son.

"I teach the pottery classes," Orin clarified. "And some of the drawing and painting classes. For beginners. They aren't my strength."

"He made all his own dishes," Lou went on. "And a lot of mine. I eat my oatmeal out of the bowl he made every morning." He grinned.

Orin didn't smile, but he seemed pleased nonetheless. When

Alex said he'd love to come by and get a tour of the Art Association, Orin told him to come by any time.

IT TURNED out that Alex's mother stayed with Lou most of the time, so Alex often felt like he had the house to himself. It worked well, since he got up and went to bed earlier than was sociable. But it was strange having so much space. Though it was his childhood home, his mom had done some renovations since he'd left, so the kitchen and living room weren't as he remembered them. After sharing New York apartments for the last ten years, the house seemed sprawling, and Alex would sometimes walk from room to room, wondering if he should rent something of his own instead. Something smaller. He didn't know if his mother would want to sell this place if she moved in with Lou definitively. Something told him she might have been waiting to see what his plans were before deciding.

But Alex wasn't sure what his plans were. Everything had been on fast-forward since leaving New York. And Son was settling into a routine, and he'd hired another baker, Hector, though he still needed to hire an assistant. It was early days, and Alex knew with nauseating clarity how many businesses failed in their first year. Still, he was cautiously optimistic.

About the business side of things, anyway.

Other things felt more unsettled. It was strange being back, and he was struggling not to feel like he'd somehow stumbled into an alternate reality in which he'd never left Ann Arbor after high school, never gone to culinary school, never worked in New York restaurants. It was strange to be in the house without his dad there. Strange to use the coffee mug he'd seen his dad use a thousand times, or rake the leaves off the front yard and realize he'd pulled on his father's gloves to do so.

His father's absence wasn't painful the way it once was, but regret welled up at the most unpredictable moments. When he came across a pun on a city sign, snuck in by someone trying to make their job a little more interesting; his father had always gotten such a kick out of those. When he realized there was something about his father's history that he didn't know, and now could never ask. When faced with a situation he knew his father would see in a way he couldn't even predict. Back in Ann Arbor, in the house he'd lived in with his father, he found these moments happening more often than they had in New York. He felt his presence a little more closely, and he welcomed it, like an unexpected gift found years after you wanted it.

Alex took to walking to And Son in the cold predawn and taking rambling walks after dinner. In New York, he'd walked everywhere, but it hadn't been the same. He'd yearned, often, for the fresh air of his youth. Now he walked through sleepy neighborhoods in the morning and tramped through the fields behind his house in the evening. He took Sunday and Wednesday mornings off, drove to the woods, and took long walks along the river.

He wanted to get a dog. It had never felt fair to get one in New York, with the hours he kept and the tiny apartments he lived in. And Timo had been anti-dog. Now, though, he could get one, and he imagined taking it with him to the river, letting it run around in the backyard. Maybe if he trained it well, it could snooze next to the counter at And Son.

The thing that felt most unsettled, though, was his response to Corbin Wale.

He couldn't stop thinking about him. Could hardly tear his eyes away when Corbin was in the bakery. It wasn't like Alex. His attractions had always been so straightforward, so measured. He felt as if he'd been jumping wavelets near the shore his whole life and now he was treading water far out at sea, his back to the impending swell.

34

Something about Corbin called to everything in him, and though Corbin wasn't an easy man to get to know, every time he walked through the door, it felt like things were right in Alex's world. He felt a kind of peace and satisfaction that came from having the person you most wanted to see near you, and Alex couldn't explain it any better than that.

Corbin had been coming in regularly the last two weeks, sometimes staying for an hour, sipping his coffee and staring into space, and sometimes sitting all day, drawing in a world of his own. He always paid attention to Alex, though, even when he ignored everyone else.

The last few days, he'd come in later in the day, and had stayed after closing. Sometimes drawing while Alex worked, sometimes talking.

Tonight they were talking while potting herbs in the windowsills. Alex wanted to have them fresh to bake with all winter. He potted basil and thyme while Corbin potted mint and rosemary.

"I could bring you some more herbs from home," Corbin offered. "Sage, lemon balm, lavender. I'm not sure what else is good for baking, but I have a lot. There's a greenhouse. I'm not very good at growing things. Not as good as my aunts were. But they're still there."

"I'd love that, thanks. You can use lots of herbs in baking. Lemon and lavender are great in cookies or cakes. Herbs like sage, chives, parsley are good in breads and other savory pastries. I really like using the ingredients as an inspiration for what to make."

Corbin ran a fingertip over the dirt in each pot, not smoothing it, just touching.

"In New York, seasonality mostly means what's cheaper to buy. I've always worked places that are operating at such a large scale they can't really source locally or be at the mercy of the weather. But now I really like that I was able to get contracts with all local providers."

Alex glanced at Corbin to see if he was interested, to find Corbin watching him intently, head slightly cocked.

"I've been going into the woods to walk, and thinking about how here it would be possible to actually use things that are in season." Alex shrugged. "Everything's different all of a sudden."

There was a line between Corbin's dark brows, but he just kept watching.

"I didn't know I'd be coming back here," Alex explained. "But I got dumped and fired in one week, and leaving New York seemed advisable before a piano fell on me or something."

Alex had been going for a light tone, but Corbin frowned.

"You got dumped. Why."

"Because . . . because my boyfriend had all these plans for our future that I knew nothing about. And when he found out I knew nothing about them, he realized that we didn't want the same things. We weren't even living in the same world."

By the time Alex got to the end of his sentence, Corbin was gone. His gaze had turned inward and his expression smoothed. He smiled vaguely at Alex before he left. Alex walked home slowly, fingers still smelling of thyme.

"HEY, CORBIN?" Alex said a few days later.

They'd just finished closing and Alex was feeling reckless. This morning he'd woken to a gust of cold air through the open window that made the whole world seem fresh and new. All day the feeling had stayed with him, a crisp sense of possibility.

"Hi." Corbin looked up. He always said *Hi* like he was reminding himself it was something he was supposed to say. The collar of his button-down denim shirt gaped as he drew, revealing

36

a glimpse of delicate collarbones that Alex couldn't tear his eyes from.

"Hi. Listen, do you think I could come home with you today?" Corbin's eyes went wide and he froze. "Thing is, I think I want a dog. I've always wanted one, and this is the first time I might be able to have one. And you said your dogs mill around. I thought maybe I could hang out for a few minutes, see if being around them seals the deal."

"To my house."

Alex nodded. "I won't come inside, if you don't want. I could just stay in the yard."

He watched Corbin closely, ready to retract the question if Corbin seemed uncomfortable, but he just seemed confused.

"No one comes to my house."

"Okay, that's fine, forget I asked." Alex smiled and started to turn away. This was what Corbin did, he'd realized. He stated things as if they were facts, but they weren't what he wanted, only what he thought he knew. If given time, though, he'd get to what he wanted.

"No, I— No, you can come. The dogs. And you—I could show you the greenhouse. If you want. Dogs." He nodded.

"Great," Alex said with a grin. "Did you walk?"

Corbin always walked.

They walked to Corbin's in silence, Alex giddy with fresh air and their destination. Corbin was clearly mulling something over. It wasn't the same as when he was lost in thought. When he was mulling, he seemed almost to vibrate. After they'd walked for twenty minutes, Corbin said, "You're gay."

"Yeah. Is that why you left the other night after I mentioned having a boyfriend?"

"No. Yes. I had to think about it," Corbin said.

"I know in high school people teased you about being gay. But kids say a lot of things that aren't true. Just so you know that I don't assume anything about you."

"I wasn't anything in high school."

"And now?" Alex asked softly.

"Now. Now I'm only me. I'll always be only me."

When they rounded the corner and cut through a copse of trees, Alex found himself faced with the scene from Corbin's sketchbook: the trees, the imposing house, the garden. He followed Corbin down the incline to the yard behind the house. Chimes hung all around the back porch, clacking in the breeze, and birds clustered around four different feeders, one of which was home to a battle between three finches and a plump brown squirrel.

As they neared the deck, a form bounded out of the trees and before he could register what it was, Alex was on his back, gazing at the sky. Then his field of vision was filled with a face he recognized from Corbin's sketchbook. Gray fur, a black nose, and chilly blue eyes.

"It's okay. He's okay," Corbin said, and the dog walked away. Alex pushed himself up on his elbows to stand, and saw Corbin kneeling on the grass next to the dog.

"Wolf is protective," he said simply.

"No kidding. I'm glad you've got him to look out for you. He isn't really a wolf, is he?"

Corbin bit his lip, and Alex wondered if he hadn't meant to share the dog's name.

"Maybe part." Corbin wrapped his arms around Wolf and buried his face in his fur. The dog—Alex was going to keep thinking of it as a dog, thank you very much—tilted his head to rest on Corbin's and put his front paws on Corbin's thigh. They stayed like that for so long Alex felt the damp of the grass soak into his jeans.

When Alex stood, Corbin reluctantly unwrapped himself from Wolf and stood as well. He whistled once, twice, then a third time, and three more dogs loped out of the woods and gathered at Corbin's feet.

Corbin called the large shaggy brown-and-white dog Cow. The small brindle dog that looked like some kind of terrier mix and kept jumping around Alex's ankles, Corbin called Snap. The third dog had sleek black fur that was missing in patches, and a torn ear. It was quiet and calm, and leaned against Corbin's legs so heavily that Alex was surprised he didn't pitch over. Corbin called it Ghost.

They stood with the dogs for a while, Alex petting them and confirming that, yes, he wished he had one. Then Corbin found a few sticks and they started throwing them for the dogs to chase. Wolf was the fastest, but lost interest once he'd found the stick, leaving Cow or Snap to bring it back. Snap jumped excitedly on the stick as Cow waited. Ghost just stood, watching it all.

After a few throws, a crash came from the trees in the other direction, and the ugliest dog Alex had ever seen made for the most recently thrown stick like a bullet. It snarfed and pawed at the stick clumsily, and let out a howl of frustration when it couldn't pick it up.

"Let me guess," Alex said. "That's Stick?"

"Yes."

"What . . . what is she doing?"

Stick was scrabbling at the ground with two paws like she was trying to hold the stick and walk on her back paws.

"When she was a puppy, Aunt Hilda's cat, Morrigan, had kittens, and Stick ran around with them all the time. She still tries to pick things up. She used to be able to. Kind of. But she's getting old now. Stick!" Corbin called, and she came galloping toward them, skidding to a halt a foot from Corbin's toes. Corbin threw another stick and Stick barked once, then shot off after it.

"I'd really like a dog," Alex said. "Maybe it could even come to the bakery." Corbin's eyes lit up at that and Alex determined he'd make it happen one way or another. "Do you train them? I don't really know much about training dogs."

"No. They're just themselves. I don't tell them what to do."

Should have seen that coming, Alex thought.

"And their names aren't Stick, Ghost, Wolf, Cow, and Snap, right?" Alex said with a smile.

"No," Corbin said, seriously. "It's just what I call them."

It was getting dark, but Stick was still enthusiastic about their game, so Alex ran to grab another stick. His foot slipped on a slick of leaves and he skidded for a moment and then landed on his knees in a slick patch of grass, his pants covered in mud that immediately soaked through.

Alex stood and wiped his muddy hands on his muddier jeans. Corbin was smiling at him.

"You okay."

"Yeah. Surely you can tell I used to play sports from my incredible coordination."

Corbin's smile was bigger than any Alex had seen from him, and it made being cold, wet, and covered in mud feel entirely worth it. It creased the taut skin around Corbin's eyes and made his nose wrinkle in a way that made him look slightly goofy and completely adorable.

"You can come inside," he said, eyeing Alex's pants. "My pants won't fit you, but I have a towel."

"Thanks."

The sun had set completely and the house was just a looming shadow one shade darker than the dark around them, but Corbin walked unerringly and Alex trailed behind him, shoes squishing in the muddy grass. Cow and Snap chased each other around the yard, and Ghost stood, watching them. Wolf walked alongside Corbin and sat down next to the door like a sentry.

"Night, Wolf," Corbin said softly. He hugged him and kissed the top of his head, and Wolf licked his cheek once, then settled in. Did he stay all night? Alex hoped so. Even though they were only about a mile and a half from his own house, it felt far more isolated out here, the house farther from its closest neighbors.

Corbin unlocked the door and flipped on the light, and Stick came bounding over. Her tongue was lolling out and her eyes went in two different directions, but as Corbin closed the door behind her, grabbed a rag that hung by the door, and began wiping the mud from her feet, she swayed in doggie delight and her tail slapped the ground as she tried to lick his hair.

Alex allowed himself to indulge briefly in the fantasy that Corbin might clean him off too.

Once her feet were clean, Stick ran off into the house. They'd entered via a small mudroom, and Alex followed Corbin through into the kitchen. Corbin flicked on the light and started filling a bowl with dog food, while Alex looked around in wonder.

The kitchen had whitewashed walls and all natural wood—broad, butcher-block countertops, beautiful hand-carved cabinetry, and thick wood flooring. It had high ceilings, and bundles of dried herbs hung around the large leaded window. There was an oven and six-burner stove that were old but appeared in good condition, with cast iron pans hung above it. On the far wall was a stone fireplace with an iron pot stand.

A large Shaker table held a hand-carved wooden bowl with a few apples and bananas in it, and a mason jar filled with pussy willow branches.

It smelled like dried sage and lemon, candle wax and a hint of woodsmoke.

"Wow," said Alex. "This is absolutely gorgeous." Alex knew a kitchen that had been built with love when he saw one.

Corbin hummed and waved him along, turning on lights as he went. As Alex followed him, he only caught glimpses of the living room and front door. At the bathroom, Corbin handed him a towel and left.

The bathroom was a strange color caught between gray and lavender with an indiscernible light gray pattern. No, not a pattern. It was pencil sketches. Someone—presumably Corbin—had drawn all over the walls. Alex could make out pinecones and acorns, leaves and clouds, cats and dogs and birds. He sat on the closed toilet seat to dry off his pants and saw that down near the baseboard were trailing roses with wicked thorns.

He could smell lavender in here, as if to match the color of the walls. The soap next to the sink looked homemade, and he sniffed it. Yes, lavender.

Once he'd cleaned up, he washed his hands with the lavender soap so he could take at least the scent of Corbin's house home with him.

"Corbin?" Alex walked back toward the kitchen, but Corbin came from the other direction. "Oh, hey. Thanks for the towel."

Corbin took it from him, and for a moment, the piece of fabric connected them. Then Alex let go and disappointment washed through him.

They walked to the front door, where the wood floor was in worse condition, with dings and dark grooves between the boards.

"Thanks again," Alex said at the door. He wanted so badly to hug Corbin, or kiss his cheek. Even a handshake would be something. But Corbin had made it clear he didn't like to be touched, and Alex shoved his hands deep in his pockets so he couldn't.

"Alex." It was, he realized, the first time Corbin had ever said his name. Corbin's voice caught on the x, making the word his own, and it hovered in the air between them. "I . . . I am."

It took Alex a moment to rewind to the question Corbin was answering.

"Okay. Do you have a boyfriend?"

"No. No, I can't." Corbin looked away.

"You can't? Why not?"

Corbin bit his lip and when he his eyes met Alex's again, he looked sad and lost. Not lost in his thoughts as he so often was, but adrift somewhere. Unmoored. Lonely.

"It's not worth it. Bad things would happen."

Chapter Five

THE PHONE CALL jolted Alex from a dead sleep. Gareth.

"Hey, what's up?"

"Are you— Did I wake you? I thought you'd be in the kitchen."

Alex peeked at his phone. It was 5:02 am. Just around the time he'd usually be getting there.

"I'm off today. Hired another baker. I'll go in this afternoon to check on everything." *Not just to see if Corbin's there.*

"God, I'm sorry. I'm sorry. I'm so sorry. I'll let you go. Sorry."

His voice was miserable and panicked in a way Alex had rarely heard it, and the back of Alex's neck prickled.

"What's wrong?"

"Um. Well. It's not . . . I . . ."

"What the fuck did he do, Gareth?" Alex growled. There was only one person who could make Gareth sound like that. Gareth's husband, Paul.

Alex hated Paul, had hated him from the first time he met him. And Alex did not hate a lot of people.

Paul was smarmy and aggressive and manipulative, and he treated Gareth as his property. Alex had been sure their relationship would never last. Surely, Gareth would call Paul on his shit and wave goodbye. Alex just had to bite his tongue until then. Only Gareth never did wave goodbye; he said, "I do," instead. In a weekend elopement that he confessed as if ashamed when he saw Alex afterward.

It had been the last straw. Alex had told Gareth exactly what he thought of Paul, and Gareth had flushed red with anger and maybe shame, and hadn't spoken to Alex for a month. It was the longest they'd ever gone without speaking, and when they'd made up—Alex apologizing sincerely, though his opinion of Paul would never change—it had been with the unspoken agreement that Alex wouldn't insult Paul again.

Alex had kept his side of that bargain, making up a bed on the couch for Gareth when he showed up with haunted eyes and bruises he covered. Pulling Gareth out of the house to go see silly action movies or drink milkshakes when he found him with tears streaking his face and his mouth set in a grim line. If that was what Gareth needed from him, then that was what he did. But he didn't have to like it, and after he walked Gareth back home, hands gentle on his friend's hair, arms soft around his shoulders, Alex would take out his aggression with hard fists on the punching bag in the gym in his building, imagining the bag was Paul's face and every punch bore his name.

He heard Gareth's breath stutter and then he heard a muffled whine.

"Gareth." Alex made his voice soft, gentle. "Talk to me, please. Tell me what happened. I can tell you're upset and you're not getting me off this phone until you tell me why. You *know* how stubborn I am. You know I'll stay on the phone all day."

Gareth started to cry—gasping sobs that turned muffled, like Gareth had put the phone down next to him. "I think—" he choked out. "I— He freaked out. He wanted me to quit my job and . . . I don't know where it came from, but once he— Fuck, I don't know, once he got it in his head, he just . . . nothing I said . . . he was so mad and he was making no sense. He said people were always looking at me, and I said no one even sees the chef and he —he—he—"

"Gareth, what happened next?"

For a moment Gareth said nothing, and Alex could hear his deep, shuddering breaths. When he spoke next, his words came out in a jumble and he sounded manic, talking about everything except the topic at hand. He talked about a customer at Rouge

44

who sent their plate back, and about a dog he'd seen in the park. Alex let him talk for a while, contemplating how terrible the food was in prison as a deterrent from catching the next flight out of Detroit and murdering Paul.

When his friend ran out of steam and started repeating "Um, um, um," over and over as if waiting for the words to come, Alex said, "I want you to send me a picture."

"Hmm? Of what?" Gareth asked breezily.

"Of you. Of what he did to you. We both know that I know."

Gareth made a horrible sound. Alex waited him out. Then the call disconnected. Alex took one deep breath, two, three. He'd call back after ten breaths if Gareth hadn't sent the picture.

At breath six, a photo lit up his phone and Alex's breath was gone. The light was dim, but Alex could see enough to be glad he was in Michigan and not able to get his hands on Paul, because he didn't trust what he might do if he could.

He called back. Gareth answered and said nothing.

"Where are you now?" Alex asked.

"Home." Gareth's voice was tiny.

"You're still there? Is he there?"

"No, he's . . . He left. After . . . last night, he left. He said he was going out for a while. I think . . . I think he frightened himself."

Alex's heart was a hummingbird. He tried not to sound as scared as he felt.

"Gareth, listen. I think it'd be a good idea if you left. Here, I'll come with you, okay? Put on some shoes and get your coat, and your wallet, and your phone charger, and take your keys. Then walk out the front door and stay on the phone with me. Okay?"

"I don't want anyone to see me like this," Gareth whispered.

"Grab that baseball cap and your sunglasses—the big ones I always tease you for wearing. Get a scarf. Take the stairs. Okay?"

Rustling sounds and then silence.

"Gareth?"

"Okay, I . . . Okay."

"Okay, let's leave. You need to leave. Now," he added, at the silence on the line.

"Okay," Gareth said again.

Gareth's breathing was loud, and Alex realized he was standing in the dark, the hand not holding the phone wrapped so tight in his bedclothes that he had no feeling in his fingers. When he heard the hollow echo of Gareth's footsteps and realized his friend was indeed taking the emergency stairs instead of the elevator, he unwound his hand from the sheets and forced himself to take a deep breath.

"I'm here, Gareth. What floor are we on?"

"Fourth," Gareth said, his voice echoing.

"Okay, that's good. Almost done. Remember that year we lived in the fourth floor walkup I sublet from Carly at school? I thought you were gonna kill me."

"I did want to kill you. But then I realized climbing all those stairs made my ass look fantastic, so I let you live."

Swing of a door and then another, and then a muffled voice that might have been the doorman, and Gareth's breath came fast, too fast.

"Where are we now? Are we outside?"

"Uh-huh."

"Okay, that's great. You're doing great."

"It's still there," he said softly.

"What is, G?"

"The apartment." His voice sounded wrong. "My life. My whole life. It's there, in that building. It's all just there. Oops, I left the light on in the bedroom . . . I should . . . maybe I should . . . I should probably—"

"*Gareth*! Listen to me. You need to leave now. You need to walk away from the building. Here, go to Ocello's, okay? They'll be open. Go to Ocello's and get a coffee and an almond croissant. That's what you get there, right? But you need to leave."

"Alex. Alex. Alex, I think . . . I need to leave."

"Yeah, that's right. You need to leave. Let's go."

"I need . . . I think I need to leave."

"Yeah, babe, I think you do."

"Oh, fuck, Alex, I gotta leave." Gareth's voice was high and thin, his teeth chattering.

The pain in Alex's chest welled into his throat and choked him. His heart was pounding so hard, he could feel its echoes through his ribcage, like the very architecture of his body couldn't contain his fear.

"Yeah, that's right," he choked out. "Let's go to Ocello's. Get two coffees—one for me, okay? Let's go. Now, okay? Now."

"Okay."

After a few seconds, Alex heard the hum of traffic and let out the breath he'd been holding.

"We almost there?" he asked.

"Yeah. Alex. I mean, I think I need to *leave*."

"Come here, Gareth. Come here."

THE NEXT MORNING found Alex in the kitchen at And Son, relieved to have only the straightforward task of baking in front of him. He hadn't made it in to work the afternoon before at all. He'd stayed on the phone with Gareth all day.

Gareth had agreed to come to Michigan for a little while, to get some distance and sort things out. But he needed to talk to his boss at Rouge, who wouldn't be happy about needing to find a sub at the last minute. Before he could think, Alex pointed out that if she took one look at him, she wouldn't hesitate to give him the time off, and immediately regretted it at the silence on the line.

It quickly became clear that Gareth didn't want *anyone* to see him. He didn't want to go into a coffee shop, he didn't want to go to work, he didn't even want to go to the airport. When Alex finally realized the depth of his repulsion, they agreed that Gareth would check into a hotel for a day or two before he flew.

By dinnertime, Alex was so exhausted that he just went back to bed. He woke up with every noise, his body primed to hear the phone. But Gareth had checked in to the hotel, and had sent Alex a picture to prove it—and to make fun of the decor, which convinced Alex he was feeling a bit more like himself.

Now, with confirmation that Gareth's plans for the day involved nothing but reality television and room service, and with his phone in clear sight next to him, Alex put flour, eggs, butter, and sugar on the worktable and breathed deeply.

A few hours later, Mira pushed through the doors. "Hey, boss, do you have—whoa. Uh. I was going to ask if you have any more croissants because we're about out." She picked up a full tray of croissants and eyed the five other things he was in the middle of. "I'll just take these. These too." She took a tray of scones and the blueberry coffee cake, and Alex went back to work.

Hours later, Mira came in again. "Holy mother of god, would you stop for a second?"

Alex glanced around and saw the table full of bread and pastries. The timer on the oven dinged and he pulled out a lemon-lavender pound cake.

Mira shook her head. "Are we expecting some kind of after-noon rush I don't know about, or are you freaking out?"

"Freaking out. Don't mind me. Here, take some ginger plum tarts home with you when you leave."

"Uh, well, I won't say no to that. You okay? You want to . . . uh, talk or . . .?"

"I'll be fine, and no, thank you." Her relief was clear. "Hey, is Corbin in today?"

Mira smirked and nodded, raising one eyebrow.

"How long's he been here?"

"Since the scones." Mira measured time based on when they put out new offerings behind the counter.

"Does it look like a long-haul kind of day?"

"Maybe. You want me to . . . give him a message or something?"

"No. I'm almost done."

"Thank god," she muttered. "Tell me what I'm selling and I'll add it to the board."

It was around three in the afternoon when Alex washed his hands, back and arms tight from working so much dough, and emerged from the kitchen. He felt better, lighter.

Corbin was wearing a moth-eaten red and blue wool sweater and his bleach-speckled black corduroys were threadbare on the knees and thighs. He looked soft and touchable, and Alex was struck with a vision of what it would be like if he had the right to enfold Corbin in his arms, nuzzle his face into the man's hair or rest his chin on his shoulder. As he'd done two nights before, Alex shoved his hands in his pockets to make sure he didn't give in to the urge to touch Corbin.

"Hi," he said, and a jolt of pleasure ran through him when Corbin's face lit up at the sight of him.

"Hi."

"How are the dogs?"

"Fine."

Corbin gestured at the drawing he was working on and pushed the notebook toward Alex. It was Wolf and the rest of the dogs, playing in the yard. But when Alex looked closer, he realized that it wasn't Corbin or any of his on-page friends that the dogs were piled on top of—it was him.

Corbin had drawn Alex half covered in dogs, but smiling. Alex took in the shine of his hair, mingled blond and light brown, the warmth in his light brown eyes. Corbin had drawn him handsome—handsomer than he was, Alex thought.

"You're really talented," Alex said. "I've always liked comics a lot. Your style reminds me a little of Fiona Shae. Do you know her stuff?" Corbin shook his head. "Really different subject matter and colors, but it's got a similar kind of dreamy, magical feel."

Corbin smiled.

"I don't want to interrupt you if you're still drawing, but I made you something. Do you want to come in the kitchen?"

"You made something specifically for me." He sounded disbelieving.

"Yeah. I don't know if you'll like it, but, yes."

He'd thought about Corbin's taste for warm spices and autumnal flavors, wanting to bake him something. Wanting to be able to give him something, since he couldn't touch him.

Corbin's eyes went wide when he saw the cake. "It's a whole cake."

"It's a carrot walnut cake with candied ginger and cardamom frosting."

"You made me a cake."

Alex suddenly felt very silly. "I did. I— You don't have to take it. I just was thinking of you. And I baked it for you."

"No one's ever made me a cake before," Corbin said.

"Not even for your birthday when you were little?"

He shook his head, then stared at Alex. "What's wrong. You're all different today."

"Bad day yesterday. My best friend in New York got hurt, and I'm not exactly sure how to help him."

"I'm sorry," Corbin said, stepping closer. Alex could smell him. A breath of fresh green nature that cut through the sweetness and yeast of the kitchen. "Will he be okay."

"I hope so."

"You . . . Did you bake me a cake because your friend was hurt."

Alex's head snapped up. "No."

But hadn't he? He'd felt unable to protect Gareth, and his mind had wandered to the way he wished he could protect Corbin, and since Corbin was as skittish as a stray, he did the only thing he could think to do. He baked.

"Well, not exactly. I baked for you because I like you and I

wanted to give you something that might make you . . . happy."
He flushed. It sounded childish.

But Corbin was blinking at him, paying attention. He opened
and closed his mouth and then he smiled, a slow, sweet smile.

"Do you want to taste it? It's okay if you don't like it."

Corbin nodded, and Alex handed him a fork. Corbin stuck the
fork in the cake like he was getting away with something. Alex
swallowed hard as he watched him eat it, struck again by the intimate pleasure of watching Corbin consume something he'd made.
Reel it in, Barrow, and stop perving on the guy eating cake.

"It's so good," Corbin murmured, and stuck the fork in again.
Alex glowed.

They talked for a while, and Alex offered to drive Corbin
home so he wouldn't have to walk while carrying the cake.

"So, do you do art for your job too?" Alex asked as they drove.

"No, I don't have a job right now. I got fired."

"You did? Why? Where were you working?"

"I don't want to talk about it right now."

"Oh," Alex said. "Okay, no problem."

He pulled up in front of Corbin's house and Corbin slid out,
clutching the cake box to his chest.

"Thank you for the cake, Alex," he said softly. And at the
sound of his name in Corbin's mouth, Alex knew the other man
had been right. Because every time Corbin uttered *Alex*, Corbin
had power over him like nothing he'd ever known.

"I DON'T SUPPOSE you'd want to work here?" Alex asked Corbin
the next day. Corbin was helping him fill an almond torte.

Corbin snorted and shook his head. "You don't want me to

work here. People think I'm weird, and they won't want to eat things I touch." He bit his lip.

"Well, it doesn't matter if people think you're weird because you'll be in the kitchen. It's a baking assistant that I need. I thought you might want to try."

"Why."

"Well, you said you don't have a job right now. And you're good at it."

"I'm not. I don't know anything about it. I just do what you tell me."

Alex grinned. "It's a good start."

The air between them sizzled.

"I—I can't . . . You can't be serious."

Alex couldn't believe how serious he was.

"I am."

"You can't," Corbin said softly. "I don't want anything bad to happen here."

"Your self-esteem isn't great, gotta say."

But Corbin just shook his head.

Neither is your sense of humor, Alex thought. There was something incredibly charming to him about the way Corbin didn't joke around. Like everything he said and thought was serious, sincere, genuine. Unguarded by the distance humor provided.

Alex's eyes lingered on the line of Corbin's neck as he dropped his head. "Corbin. Do you *want* to?"

He nodded. "I want to."

Alex grinned. It felt like a piece had slid into place in a puzzle, though he didn't know what the final picture would be.

CORBIN *WAS* GOOD AT IT. He paid attention to detail, he followed instructions well, and he never assumed that he knew anything he didn't know. It was as good a place to start as any.

Alex's one reservation about hiring Corbin had been the way the man got lost in his own thoughts. He feared he might let trays burn or leave dough proofing for days. Instead, Corbin turned that absorption to whatever he was working on. So Alex was treated to that same single-minded focus on creaming butter and sugar, on evenly strewing berries in custard, on forming perfect rolls.

In fact, it was Alex's thoughts that had a tendency to wander when Corbin was in the kitchen, Alex who nearly burned three things and found two tubs of over-risen dough on Corbin's first day. *Get it together, get it together, get it together*, he scolded himself.

Corbin was careful not to touch him all day, but as they moved around each other in the kitchen, Alex's awareness of the other man's body was so heightened that it felt like they touched anyway. The air between them was charged, and when he'd catch a hint of Corbin's scent, Alex would feel his body flood with desire.

It was almost a relief when afternoon rolled around and Corbin's trial shift was over. Alex was leaving also, to go pick up Gareth from the airport.

"You did really well," Alex said. "Did you like it?" Corbin grinned and nodded quickly. "Okay, then. You're hired."

ALEX HAD snuck glances at Gareth all the way from the airport. He thought he could see concealer on what he remembered to be the worst of the bruises, but nothing could have hidden the still-unhealed split lip or the puffiness around his left eye. After fifteen minutes, Gareth had smacked him in the shoulder and told him to cut it out because he felt like enough of a loser without being gawked at.

Back home, Gareth had flung his suitcase into the guest room and slumped moodily on the couch. Every time Alex tried to talk about anything more substantial than the show Gareth had chosen on the Cooking Channel, Gareth fobbed him off. Alex was starting to get irritated.

This was what Gareth did when he felt threatened or judged, Alex knew that very well. But he wanted so much to help, and he'd been so worried for days, and now Gareth had fifty things to say about mirepoix and nothing to say about himself. Even "How are you?" had only garnered a snort.

But Gareth straightened from his slouch when the door opened and Alex's mom came in. Alex had asked her if it was all right for Gareth to stay for a while, but he hadn't told her the details of why. She came into the living room with a smile, but it melted away the moment she saw Gareth.

"Hi, Helen," Gareth said quietly, eyes downcast, like he was about to be scolded. He looked guilty. The first time Alex's mother had come to visit, Gareth had said, awed, "So that's what having a real mom is like?"

She sat on the couch next to Gareth. She considered him for a moment, reaching out to touch his cheekbone where the concealer was thick and obvious. Gareth let her, where he'd slapped Alex's hand away. She let out a sigh and held open her arms. "Come here, sweetie," she said.

Gareth's eyes flicked up to hers and then he threw himself into her arms sobbing.

Alex watched in shock as Gareth cried and his mother stroked his hair and his back. And he tried not to feel hurt when his mom shooed him away from his best friend.

He grabbed his coat off the peg and walked into town. When

he got back with Chinese takeout two hours later, Gareth was nowhere to be seen.

"He went to bed," Helen said quietly, coming into the kitchen and helping herself to some food.

"He wouldn't even tell me how he was," Alex said. It sounded bitter.

"Sometimes people just need a mom."

Alex blinked at her. "Yeah, I guess so." They ate in silence for a minute. "What do you do when you need one?" His mother's parents were both long dead.

Helen pursed her lips and smiled a little. "It's the strangest thing. Once you become a mom, you need one differently." She smiled at him and put a hand on his shoulder. "You did a good thing, bringing him here."

"I hope so. I'm not really sure what to do now that he's here."

She shrugged. "Most people don't know what they're doing most of the time. You'll figure it out."

It was something she'd said to him so many times when he was growing up, but it hit him differently this time.

"Yeah. I guess I will," he said.

ON HIS WAY home from And Son the next day, Alex stopped at the grocery store and got boxed macaroni and cheese, bacon, limes, and tequila. He set these things on the kitchen table and woke Gareth, who'd been dozing on and off all day.

"Wow, you're the devil," Gareth said when he saw.

"I need to talk to my best friend and my best friend likes bacon mac and cheese when he drinks." Alex shrugged. "You do the math."

Gareth's nostrils flared, and he said sharply, "I don't want to talk about this shit, Barrow."

"Psh, who's talking about you, I'm talking about me," Alex said, putting water on to boil. He sliced a lime and poured them each a tumbler of tequila, then he handed one to Gareth and clinked.

Gareth threw back the tequila and swore a blue streak when the liquor burned his split lip. He stuck his finger in the olive oil and swiped it across his mouth.

"Okay, what the fuck do you want to talk about?"

Alex dumped the boxes of macaroni in the water and relished the sizzle of the bacon as it hit the pan.

"So, there's this guy," he said. And he watched the life come back to Gareth's face for the first time since he'd arrived.

Part Two ❧ Water

Corbin

Chapter Six

ALEX BARROW HAD STREAKED into Corbin's life like a shooting star through a dark sky. Things that had long dwelt in shadow were illuminated. Things that had been buried deep could no longer be ignored.

The morning he met Alex, Corbin had woken from a dream of swans roosting in the eaves, their feathers falling like snow. He'd pushed the window open and smelled apples on the air. Green apples and moss. They were the scents of possibility, and he'd set out walking without knowing where they'd take him.

When he'd gotten to Helen's place and the scent dissipated, he was a bit disappointed. Not that he didn't like Helen's coffee shop —it was where he always went. But the smell had been so fresh and sharp that he'd thought it meant something different. He'd told himself it had just been a sign that the coffee shop was open again, after weeks of being closed. At least, he'd thought it was weeks. Corbin wasn't great with time.

It was only when he'd walked in that he'd realized everything was different. The man at the counter had a warm glow around him. It felt like kindness and nature and energy and something Corbin didn't quite recognize. Something he couldn't look away from.

It was like desperation but with none of the darkness.

Now, Corbin knew that his first impression of Alex had been correct. He was kind to his core, with boundless energy to take on a project, and he savored fresh air and trees as if each breath were the first he'd had in a long while. He reminded Corbin a little bit of Wolf.

But there was still the quality he couldn't figure out. It wasn't sadness—not exactly. Nor loneliness. There was no pity to it, no regret. The closest Corbin could name it was something like potential. An unused resource. Something waiting for . . . something.

CORBIN FLOATED home at the end of his first week officially working as a baker at And Son, mind still on the transformation of heat and yeast. Wolf bounded up to him excitedly and nuzzled him, taking in all his new scents.

"Come walk with me." Wolf fell into step with him.

They walked into the woods, Corbin trailing his fingers along pine needles and pressing close to smell bark and berries. It was the smells he missed most in the winter. The cold dulled them down so his world felt smaller, closer. He had to get right up close to things to get their full picture in winter.

He wondered if Alex liked the winter. If he'd bundle up and keep walking outdoors, or shiver and complain about the cold. Did he turn up the heat or pile extra blankets on the bed? Did he do what Corbin did, and leave the window open even through the deepest snows and most biting winds?

When his stomach growled loudly enough that Wolf turned to him with perked ears, Corbin realized he'd been walking a lot longer than he'd intended. The paths he'd worn through these woods over the years snaked into one another so that, if you weren't paying attention, you could move through them for hours without coming out the other side.

He'd been so lost in his thoughts about Alex that it had grown dark without him noticing.

"Let's go home."

Wolf barked once, and turned to the right. He would lead them unerringly home.

Corbin fixed dinner and ate at the kitchen table where he'd eaten thousands of times before. His aunts had never kept regular schedules, so cooking smells would waft through the house at all hours of the day or night, and Corbin would come to eat. Sometimes he'd awake in the middle of the night to find every pan and pot dirty and the aunts feasting at a table covered in dishes; sometimes it was freshly baked bread and butter, sometimes ice cream for days.

Whatever the whims of his aunts, there had always been food in the house if Corbin wanted to make what he liked. But he enjoyed the surprise. He would stay in his room until the last possible moment, tasting the air and making guesses about what he'd find in the kitchen.

After dinner, Corbin settled into the armchair in the living room where Stick dozed in front of the fire, paws twitching in her dreams. He opened his sketchbook and unzipped his pens, flipping pages. The last five pages featured a new subject.

Alex.

One he'd let Alex see—him smothered in dogs, alight with the joy of them. Others he hadn't.

Alex baking, strong arms tensed as he worked the dough.

Alex holding out the perfectly frosted cake that he'd made just for Corbin with a smile. Corbin had put the cake in the freezer to eat bites of when he wanted.

Alex walking with Corbin and Carbon, Lex, Jasmine, Finnian, and Wolf in the woods behind his house, as if he'd always been a part of the group.

And one that he'd never show him. One he could hardly bear to look at, himself. He'd woken from dreams of Alex and drawn it half-asleep, in the middle of a long, dark night. Alex, in Corbin's bed, arms wrapped around him, chin on his shoulder. Alex holding him, wanting him. Cherishing him.

Corbin flipped to a new page. It would never happen, so it was better to put it out of his mind. That way lay madness. Better not to want things. Better to focus on what he had instead of what he never would.

He began to draw. His tougher twin, Carbon, emerged first, glaring at him as she played with Wolf. Then elfin, blonde Lex, who'd stayed child-sized even after he'd grown up. She smiled at him like she always smiled at him. Tall, placid Jasmine strode through the woods toward them, hand raised in greeting. She didn't seem upset, just in a hurry.

Finnian was last. His handsome face held concern, but no resentment, and his hand reached out to take Corbin's. It was a relief.

"I'm sorry I haven't been around as much lately," Corbin said, running his fingertips over them once the ink was dry. "I got a new job. I think this one might be different. Well. *Alex* is different. So maybe that means the job will be too."

The fire crackled and Stick wheezed peacefully in sleep. The wind outside rustled dry leaves and the air inside smelled of pine and dried sage and tomato from his dinner. He was warm and comfortable, and he lost himself in the world that unfolded in his sketchbook.

He'd begun drawing them when he was twelve, the year he started sixth grade and his aunts were forced to send him to a real school. He should be excited, the social worker had told him—all those other kids his own age to play with, and all those things to learn! And he had been excited initially. Corbin liked new things, he just didn't get the chance for them very often.

But his excitement hadn't lasted long. His classmates were curious at first, but curiosity transmuted so effortlessly into suspicion, and *What's his deal* quickly became *What a freak*.

He could see their anxiety spike when he came near them. Not fear of him but fear of having to interact with him. Fear of the awkwardness that would come from being seen with him. And if curiosity became suspicion, fear became anger. If he sat at their lunch table and they didn't want him there, then they had to be mean and tell him to leave. And they hated him for it. If they were paired with him in history class and their friends made easy jokes about it, then they were angry with him for providing the fodder.

It was misplaced anger at themselves, but then, it nearly always was.

And it didn't matter anyway, because it affected Corbin the same. Made him feel jittery and jangly and too full of the world. Made his feet clumsy and his fingers shake and his eyes unsure where to land. Made him want to crawl under the covers where no one could see him and stay there until things were different.

He said nothing at home, until one day, Aunt Hilda found him in the forest when he was supposed to be at school. He'd left the house at the usual time, then doubled back to spend the day in the woods. Hilda never ventured into the woods alone if she could help it, but Ramshackle, one of her older and more esteemed cats, had run into the tree line, and Hilda had deigned to follow and lure her home.

It hadn't been difficult to get out of him what the trouble was, and Hilda took him home and settled him at the kitchen table while she mixed teas.

"Fear," she'd said, "is natural. But anger is the weak mind's attempt at inoculation against fear. Don't pay any attention to them. They have small minds and they'll have small lives."

"Don't we have kind of a small life," Corbin had asked, indicating the house, the garden, and the woods, which were the extent of Hilda and Jade's world.

"First, we have three lives because we're three people. And second, don't believe for one second that scope is measured in square miles."

Corbin had sighed. He'd known what she meant. Corbin wasn't as literal as people thought he was. Sometimes he just needed to limit the number of options his mind processed at one time. But he'd hoped that maybe, just this once, Aunt Hilda

63

would empathize instead of prophesy. Exclaim, *Those little assholes!* Or say, *I'm sorry, Corbin. I'm sorry that happened to you.*

But his aunts were never sorry for anything. They didn't believe in regret. And *sorry* was just a wish about something that had already happened. Just a regret on someone else's behalf.

He'd drawn Carbon that night. He'd begun sketching himself. Had meant to draw himself differently. Not because he wished he were different (*regret is useless*), but because he wondered what his life would be like if he were.

They teased him for being scrawny and clumsy, for looking like a girl; they teased him for staring too much and for not making eye contact. They made fun of his clothes because they were all the colors of the forest. They teased him for not talking, and for anything he said.

So he'd meant to draw a different version of himself, just to see. But what he'd drawn was Carbon. She wrenched herself out of his pen and onto the page, and she stared at him with her hands on her hips and her head cocked, a mirror image of his own. And she said, *Screw those little assholes, bro. Screw them and their boring-ass friends.* Then she smirked and her teeth were even sharper than his.

He slept that night with the drawing under his pillow, as if perhaps in dreams she might merge with him and make him fiercer.

But come morning, she was still there, if slightly wrinkled, and when Corbin looked in the mirror, he saw what he'd always seen. Too-large eyes, a too intent stare, and delicate bones that made him, yes, look like he could be a girl. He sighed. He hadn't thought anything would be different, but he realized in that moment that he must have hoped.

And then he heard Carbon's voice in his head (though she hadn't called herself that yet), and she said, *Duh, you look like me, bro. Which is awesome. Lucky you.* Corbin felt lighter immediately, and when he smiled, he thought his teeth were a little sharper too.

He'd put the drawing in his pocket and carried it to school with him that morning, and had ever since.

With Carbon there, he had someone to talk to, someone looking over his shoulder who could roll her eyes and laugh with him. She wasn't there all the time. *Why the hell would I want to chill at math class, bro?* But she was there enough.

Jasmine came next, about six months later. Corbin read a book featuring her, *Melt Away Homeward.* In it, a woman—Jasmine Aweke—hid on a spaceship bound for the planet where her sister, who had disappeared the year before, had last been seen. She fought in an interplanetary war, only to find that her beloved sister was leading the army for the opposing side. She was strong and confident and loyal, and Corbin admired her completely. He read the book a dozen times and images of Jasmine began working their way into his drawings. He went to her for advice and liked to walk with her in silence.

Next were Wolf and Lex. They appeared at the same time because Wolf was dragging Lex out of a stream when Corbin found them. She was giggling too hard to grab at the shoreline, jubilant and unafraid. It had been Carbon who wanted her. Carbon found Jasmine stern and distant, and she thought Lex seemed fun. But Corbin had warmed to Lex too. She was forever laughing, and when she was laughing, nothing in the world could harm her. She made Corbin laugh at himself, and in those moments, he felt impervious too.

Wolf quickly become Corbin's companion, rarely leaving his side. He was a guardian and a protector, and whenever Corbin needed him, he was there.

They got on like that for a few years. Then, when Corbin was fifteen, Finnian came. Finnian didn't talk much, but he was handsome and brave and he listened to what Corbin had to say.

He held Corbin's hand, even when Corbin's fingers trembled, and he kissed Corbin's cheek at night before he fell asleep. One night, Corbin asked where he went when Corbin was sleeping, and Finnian tapped Corbin's temple and said, *I'm always in here with you.* "Then stay tonight," Corbin had said, patting the bed beside him. "Please stay." And Finnian had stayed, a warm weight next to him while he slept. Not every night, because he didn't want the pleasure of it to wear off. Just when he really needed it.

After that, they were always together. Carbon, Jasmine, Lex, Wolf, Finnian—there, with him in his pocket everywhere he went.

When people at school teased him, he went away in his head where Jasmine would calm him down, or Carbon would curse them out. Where Lex would jolly him into good humor, or Wolf would run him ragged in the woods. Or, best of all, Finnian would kiss him sweetly until he forgot that anything else existed.

He didn't tell his aunts about them—especially about Finnian. Not because they would think what his classmates thought—that he was a freak who talked to people who weren't there—or what was quickly becoming clear his teachers and the school counselors thought—that he was mentally unstable. No, Corbin didn't tell the aunts because he knew what they'd say.

They'd tell the same stories they'd told since he was a little boy and he first asked why they weren't married. The same stories they'd told when he asked what happened to his own parents.

Davey, the love of Aunt Hilda's life, had died in the Marines, when he was twenty-two. Aunt Jade's wife had died six months to the day after their wedding, even though they'd had it in secret so no one—not even Hilda—would know. She'd been twenty-seven, healthy as anything, and had died of a heart attack in her sleep.

His parents had met canoeing around the Pictured Rocks, and fallen in love on the banks of Lake Superior. They'd shared whiskey, a tent, and a week of canoeing, and, drunk with love but restless, had planned to meet at the mouth of that same river the next year and do it all over again. Two months after their trip, when Madeleine had realized she was pregnant, she'd tried to find the man she'd met. And find him she had. In the obituary section of the *Detroit Free Press*. He'd died of an aneurism the week before.

Corbin, you see, was a Wale. And the Wales were cursed. Anyone who loved them, and whom they truly loved, died within a year.

So there was no point telling them about Finnian, nor about any other man, because Corbin could never fall in love. Not with someone who might love him back, anyway, because falling in love meant dooming his beloved to certain death.

He'd had a few encounters here and there—a few kisses, a few offers. But though he craved closeness and the feel of another's hands on his skin, the encounters left him jangled, and wanting something else entirely, and he'd stopped even considering them years ago.

In that way, the fact that most people thought he was a freak made it easier to keep his distance. Not to accidentally connect. Besides, he had Finnian when he needed him, and Finnian was lovely. Lovely and impervious.

No one else had ever really caught his fancy in that way. No one had made much of a positive impression. No one had made their way inside the walls of his attention, or his home, or his dreams. No one had begun working their way into the fantasies where only Finnian had dwelt for over a decade.

No one until Alex Barrow.

Chapter Seven

FOR THE FIRST time in his life, Corbin felt like maybe he could belong. In the kitchen with Alex, sugar between his fingers, he felt at home. Every time Alex looked up at him and smiled, or moved next to him to show him how to shape a dough or mix a batter, he felt another piece fall into place, another chime sound. The air between them danced and burned.

That was how it happened, his aunts had always told him. First you fit together so perfectly there were no seams. Then you were torn apart forever.

They were putting pastries in the display case and Alex's forearm brushed against his. Corbin shuddered. His entire skin felt hypersensitive these days. Every touch felt like a caress, every accidental press of flesh like an embrace. He thought if Alex ever actually kissed him, he might come on the spot. He always pulled away quickly, afraid to leave a blight on Alex.

Corbin dropped a muffin on the floor. *Trouble's coming.*

Mac strode through the door.

Mac thought he was a freak. *Jinx.* That's what Mac used to call him. Corbin gathered the crumbs of the pear streusel muffin.

"Alex, hello!" Mac's voice scraped at the inside of Corbin's head. "I wanted to talk to you about our Thanksgiving week Main Street promotions. Everyone's participating, but I haven't heard back from you. Did you get my email?"

"I did. Sorry not to have written you back sooner—new business and all, you understand." Alex's voice stroked Corbin's nerves back into place. "I'm not going to be participating in the Thanksgiving week activities, but thanks for the head's up."

"What? Why not?"

"Because I don't celebrate Thanksgiving, and I'm not comfortable having my business make money from it."

Alex's voice was calm, but Corbin could see his frustration, his distaste. The air around Mac muddied, and Corbin took a step backward.

"Why not? You don't have to believe in all that stuff about the pilgrims and the first Thanksgiving. Most people don't. Nowadays it's more just a time to celebrate with family, be thankful for everything we have."

"I think you're right about what the holiday means to a lot of people. That they agree it isn't celebrating anything that should be celebrated but they do it anyway. Because they don't want to disappoint loved ones or they want to take advantage of a day off from work. But honestly, Mac, the only way to encourage people to stop celebrating it is . . . well, to stop celebrating it. So, I'm sure you'll understand why I can't be a part of any Thanksgiving week promotions."

Corbin felt a smile tug at his lips. Alex's fierceness, his conviction, stirred the air between him and Mac to a swirl of abject brown and glowing purple. The purple shuddered up Corbin's spine and made him long for it to be Alex's touch instead. But Mac's brown froze him.

"Uh, yes, I suppose so."

"I have a counter-proposition, though. Perhaps you and all the other small business owners could join me in donating half our profits made during that week to some Michigan area First Nations charities?"

"Ah. Well, the promotions are already set up, so . . ."

Alex nodded knowingly. "Maybe next year."

Corbin had wanted to stay crouched behind the counter out of sight until Mac left, but a timer went off in the kitchen, so he stumbled to his feet, pan in hand. Mac's frown fell on him, and he felt insects under his skin.

"Wale. Do you *work* here, now?"

Corbin watched as Mac's outlines shifted at the sight of him. *Anger, disgust, revulsion. He hates you.*

Corbin shuffled past him and made for the kitchen, the beep of the timer like a friendly voice calling him home. He slid the almond torte out of the oven to cool and waited for Alex to come tell him what to do next.

Just the thought of Alex telling him what to do calmed Corbin.

But his calm evaporated when he saw that Mac was still talking to Alex. Because he knew what Mac would be saying. He would confide in him—*from one business owner to another.* He would warn him about Corbin. He would tell Alex that Corbin was untrustworthy, a space cadet. A freak.

Sometimes you can call his name for a full minute without him hearing you. Sometimes he doesn't show up to work at all. And then there's the way bad things follow him everywhere he goes. Mrs. Edelman's freezer exploded. Mr. Sakaturi's shop got broken into. My car caught on fire after he unloaded it. Everyone knows he ruins whatever he touches, so look out.

When Alex walked into the kitchen, Corbin looked up to see that he'd poured two dozen zucchini muffins and sprinkled the tops with pepitas and brown sugar without noticing.

For the next few minutes, Alex worked and Corbin writhed. The world had narrowed to a tunnel. At one end of it was the warmth and comfort of Alex and his kitchen, and at the other end was Corbin and the life he'd had before. He could try to pick his way through the tunnel, but it was long and sloped uphill. Or he could turn away and settle in with what he already had.

He was so tired.

"I should go," Corbin said finally, as the first tendrils of vanilla and cinnamon snaked to his nose from the muffins in the oven.

Alex glanced at the clock and frowned. "Do you feel okay? You've got two hours left on your shift."

Corbin's mouth was dry, and he swallowed convulsively. Whatever magic it was that saw, in the bland woodiness of raw zucchini, the potential for the melting sweetness of zucchini muffins, that was the magic Corbin needed.

"No, I feel okay. But I can imagine what Mac said. I thought you wouldn't want me to work here anymore."

Alex frowned, and Corbin looked at his shoes.

"What did you imagine he said?"

Corbin longed to have Wolf at his side. He always felt steadier when he could lean into Wolf's warm fur. "That I'm a freak. A weirdo. A jinx. That I ruin things. Break things. That I'm bad luck to have around, and you don't need any bad luck."

Then Alex was right there, closer than he usually came. Corbin shrank away like he always did. The last thing he wanted was to touch Alex's bare skin and risk tainting him. Risk somehow allowing the curse to rub off on him. But where Alex usually pulled back too, as if he could sense that Corbin was dangerous, this time he took Corbin's shoulders in his hands.

"I don't care what Mac says. I don't care much what most people say. You're enjoying working here, aren't you?"

It was difficult to think with Alex touching him, like all the places they touched throbbed with awareness.

"It's the best thing in my life," Corbin said, scattered and abstract, and watched the fierceness in Alex's eyes fall away and his mouth soften.

Then Alex pulled him against his broad chest—slowly, so there was time to get away. But Corbin didn't want to get away. He wanted to be enfolded, consumed, engulfed. He wanted to be held at the eye of the storm, and let the world rage around him.

In Alex's arms, time was measured in breaths and distance in the wrinkles of the clothing between them. Though he was held firmly, his breath felt deeper, like his lungs could expand up to his throat and down to his stomach, filling him with all the air he'd need to stay there forever. In Alex's arms, nothing else could touch him.

What if I could have this. What if this were possible. What if I could keep him.

There was no point asking questions if you already knew the answers. Then, questions were just regrets directed at the future rather than the past.

Because he couldn't have this. This wasn't possible. He couldn't keep him.

He was a Wale, and Wales were cursed. It was the one immutable truth he'd always known.

He took one last deep breath, to impress the feeling of Alex's arms on his bones, imprint the sensation of Alex's skin against his own, catalogue the smell of Alex's hair and breath. It was better than nothing. But in doing so, he pressed his face closer to Alex's shoulder, and Alex's arms came around him even tighter —a trap laid with the most tempting bait and teeth of snapping steel.

"Corbin," Alex whispered.

His name. His name with everything in it.

And for just a moment Corbin saw how it could happen. Saw how quickly one of the pieces could slide, and you could say, *I don't care if it ends, as long as I can have it now.* Saw that if he leaned back only a very little and tipped his face up toward Alex's, he would be kissed.

Alex would kiss him, and he would be gone, and anything would feel justifiable. He saw how his aunts must have sealed the fates of their lovers though they knew the stories better than anyone. How his mother might have convinced herself to take a chance.

He saw the monsters that love and longing could make, and they all had human faces.

"Hey, you're okay," Alex said, and Corbin realized he was shaking. He pulled away and scanned the air around Alex desperately, to make sure the colors hadn't dimmed, hadn't absorbed any of his taint.

He gathered his words up like spilled acorns and tried to put them in order, but before he could, Alex was talking again.

"So then it's settled. You're not going anywhere, and the next time Mac or anyone else has something to say about you, just don't worry about it. Okay?"

Corbin found himself nodding because Alex was a *force*. Not as strong a force as the curse, but strong. And because all that mattered was more minutes with Alex, more hours.

"Do you want to help me with this new recipe? I could use a taste tester."

Corbin nodded.

"I'm going to start making challah to sell on Fridays for Shabbat, and I have a recipe I usually use, but I wanted to try a couple of variations. One with figs and honey, and one with sundried tomatoes and basil."

Corbin nodded again.

Alex paused and looked like he was about to say something, but then he just smiled and got out what they'd need. He seemed more natural in motion.

As Alex mixed ingredients and kneaded dough, making one challah after another, he talked. He always talked as he worked. Sometimes he talked to Corbin, sometimes to what he was making, and sometimes Corbin got the sense he was just leaking words like a waking dream, letting them out so they didn't gum up the works. Alex was a well-functioning machine.

Now he talked about Mac, about Thanksgiving, about small business practices and how sick it made him that people cared more about making more money than about doing the right thing.

"It's a holiday that glorifies an American holocaust," Alex said passionately as he tore basil. "Yeah, we've turned it into something that we say is about giving thanks, so no one can argue it's bad. But that makes it even worse. Anything that we do to celebrate it only adds to the problem. There's no way I'm trying to *encourage* people to spend money because of it."

Corbin sat on a stool next to the table and listened, eyes half closed. He found Alex's voice lulling, even at a rant. It reminded him of how Finnian would tell him stories some nights, or how he'd fall asleep to Lex and Carbon debating one thing or another.

He didn't notice he'd dropped off, head on his hand, until he almost fell off the stool.

"My mom used to say I could talk someone to death, but I've never actually seen it come quite that close to happening. You okay?"

Corbin muttered that he was and stood up.

"If you promise not to fall asleep in the middle, I'll show you how to braid challah."

"Please."

Braiding interested Corbin. His aunts always said braiding was meditative. They wove baskets and knotted rope to hang bird feeders. They threaded ribbons through the hems of their skirts and braided sections of their hair at the new moon to anchor thoughts in the dark.

"Do you know how to do a three-strand braid? Okay, then we'll do six-strand braids."

Corbin watched as Alex's strong hands made sense of the snakes of dough, winding them together neatly, saying the pattern out loud as he went: *Over two, under one; over two, under one.*

"My grandmother always made challah for Shabbat and dropped it off at our house. She said braided bread was a symbol of love because it's like arms interlocking."

"Did she teach you to bake."

"Yeah. At first I wasn't interested. Then, one day, I watched her make pizza dough. I watched her the way you watched me the first day you came in here. I was transfixed by that moment. That moment where things that were completely different came together to be one thing. It was like magic." He chuckled. "My grandmother just thought I really loved pizza. Which, for the record, I really do."

When Alex smiled at him easily, Corbin felt it in his gut like a bolt of lightning.

Then Alex braided the fig and honey, and draped both with towels to rise again. He told Corbin all about challah and the different styles of braids, and about Shabbat.

When the loaves were in the oven, Alex turned to him. "I don't remember that much about you in high school." His voice was deliberately neutral. "But I remember—"

"What a freak I was," Corbin murmured.

Alex's gaze was sharp. "No. I was going to say how brave you were."

"What, why."

Alex's shame was a sour streak that wrinkled Corbin's nose. "Because you were all alone, and small, but you still didn't deny who you were. I was on the damn football team and the track team. I had friends who would've had my back. And I still didn't own who I was."

Corbin's heart pounded at the unfamiliar characterization. "But you knew."

"Yeah. I always knew. Maybe I even wished that someone would ask me directly. Because I doubt I would've been able to lie about it to someone's face. But no one ever did."

"Sometimes knowing it yourself is enough."

"Sometimes," Alex allowed. "But this was just me being scared and self-conscious. It was me valuing the wrong things. I try very hard not to do that anymore." His jaw was set and Corbin could see the truth of it. Could see the fierceness with which Alex always did what he thought was right.

It had never occurred to Corbin to deny that he was gay. But it hadn't been out a sense of righteousness. The other kids at school had called him a lot of things—some true, some not—but there had been no utility in commenting on them. They hadn't cared about the truth of him. He'd been a stand-in, a convenient spot in the universe to direct the feelings they hadn't wanted to hold inside themselves. What good would it do a spot in the universe to say if those feelings were true or false.

But Alex had looked at him and seen something different. Alex had been seeing his *own* failings in contrast, but he'd seen bravery nonetheless. It warmed Corbin to imagine that decades-old regard shining on him like a stray ray of sunlight through the small windows in their high school hallways.

The timer dinged and the smell of the challah made Corbin's stomach growl. Alex was describing a sundried tomato bread he'd had in Italy, as he let the challah cool a bit, then he cut them both slices.

Corbin's mind was still on the way Alex's arms had felt around him, when he looked up to find Alex making a face.

"Yikes," Alex said, snorting. "That doesn't work at all." He pinched off a piece and tasted it again. "I should've cleansed myself or something after that conversation with Mac. My grandmother always said don't bake while you're angry or sad because your bitterness will flavor the bread. You should bake with love if you're baking for people you love, and they'll taste the sweetness." He winked and it blasted through Corbin like a shot.

Corbin blinked, the world shifting into slow motion, tumblers falling into place. Alex was rewriting his recipe aloud—sundried tomato *pesto*, with thyme instead of basil, running in a ribbon through the challah—but Corbin's mind was racing.

Your bitterness will flavor the bread.

Negative feeling transferred into the food, communicated through its creation. If it was possible to channel bitterness and anger *into* the challah, was it possible to rid yourself of them that way, too? To bake them out of yourself? A purgation in flour and salt?

If it were possible . . . could Corbin do it? Bake the curse out of himself, one loaf at a time?

The thought ricocheted around his head, fizzed at the back of his throat, and settled in his nose, smelling of pine and snow— smelling of the kind of wildness that made things happen, and leaving him lightheaded with a surge of something that felt frighteningly like hope.

Chapter Eight

CORBIN AWOKE from the twist of a dream, gasping. He pushed himself up on trembling arms to reattach to the real. It was dark. Cold air gusted through the open window. He could smell himself in the warm tangle of bedding—his woodsy sleeping scent, and the salt-sharp tang of desire.

He let himself collapse back onto the mattress, arms outflung as bits of the dream came back. Vignettes of Alex and him would never happen in the waking world.

Alex's arms tightening around his shoulders in a hug that relaxed into simply holding each other. Alex's nose buried in his hair. Alex's fingers skimming his spine. A playful shoulder bump that turned to Alex's arm sliding around his waist to tug him close. He and Alex touching at thigh, hip, shoulder, leaning into one another like they had magnets polarized beneath their skin.

"It's not real," Corbin whispered in the dark. "It won't ever be real, so stop it." The dampness on his lashes was quickly absorbed by his hair and the pillow, and he pulled the covers back around him. He inhaled and an ocean of loneliness opened in his gut. *Finnian, I need you*, he thought, but then changed his mind. It *wasn't* Finnian he needed. Wasn't Finnian he dreamt about, his sleeping mind admitting what his waking thoughts refused.

That he wanted Alex. He wanted Alex with a fierce desperation that made him shudder in the night.

Eyes squeezed tightly shut, jaw set against the things that could never be, Corbin fell asleep and dreamt of nothing.

THE MOON CAST shadows like arrows on the sidewalk as Corbin let himself into the bakery at midnight. He got out yeast, flour, eggs, oil, and salt, measuring as Alex had.

As he kneaded the dough, he summoned everything he felt about the curse. He thought of the first time his aunts had told him of it. *The Wales are cursed in love.* Long before it could be a disappointment, it was simply a fact. *This is how things are, and this is how they can never be.*

He thought of the first time it had truly meant something. The afternoon the angle of Denny Dermott's chin and the laughing curve of his eyelashes had sent heat fluttering through Corbin's chest. He'd been fourteen, and on the walk home from school, he'd imagined kissing that chin, licking those eyelashes. Then, with a sinking sensation, he'd realized what would happen after. Not with Denny, perhaps. Or the next boy, or the next. But eventually.

As flakes of early snow stung his heated cheeks, he'd realized in a rush that wanting to kiss a boy's chin meant that eventually there might be a boy he'd love. Eventually there might be a boy whose chin he wanted to kiss forever. As the factual *how things are* turned to the personal *how they can never be*, something opened up inside Corbin that had gaped ever since.

The promise of loneliness wasn't the same as loneliness itself. Corbin knew, because it was the promise of loneliness that descended that day. It was loneliness itself that he'd felt over the last few years. Loneliness that ached with the throb of a thousand hearts. Loneliness that turned certain parts of himself to stone to stop that throbbing ache because it was easier to cut some things off than to feel the pain of them.

Corbin watched as the dough inflated with everything he wished he could throw away. Once it had risen, he rolled it into six strands. *Braids can trap ill wishes and keep them away.* He braided slowly, sending the curse into the braid.

Then he set the oven as high as it would go, and burnt the ill-wish bread to carbon.

At work later, he touched Alex's bare arm with his fingertips, raising the hairs on his own arm with the contact. For the next hour, he watched closely, waiting to see some sign that anything had rubbed off, the taint in him transferring to Alex. When nothing seemed to change, he breathed deeply.

Maybe, if he did it again and again—leached the curse out of himself and burnt it, one loaf at a time—he could be free. Maybe, just maybe, he wouldn't have to be alone forever.

IN THE BATH THAT NIGHT, Corbin closed his eyes and waited to disappear.

Finnian, he murmured, and lay motionless until the air changed.

Finnian didn't touch him; Finnian told him how to touch himself. That was the way Corbin liked it. That was the way it had always been—Finnian using him as an instrument of his own pleasure. Finnian liked to watch, and Corbin liked the way being worth watching made him feel momentarily beautiful.

When it was Finnian, it wasn't fantasy, wasn't masturbation. It was sex with someone he knew and trusted calling all the shots. Pushing him in different directions but always keeping him safe.

When he opened his eyes, Finnian was perched on the edge of the tub, languidly trailing his long fingers in the bathwater and making Corbin shiver at the thought of what those fingers would describe.

Touch your stomach lightly, under the water. Feel how slick your skin is.

Corbin shuddered at his own touch. His skin was often so sensitive that a caress of his stomach or his thigh could have him achingly hard. Sometimes brushing the inside of his biceps or under his arms made him quake with awakened desire. Once, Finnian had made him come by scratching the creases where thighs met groin, little fingers of electricity zinging everywhere.

Beneath the water, he slid his hand over his chest to circle his nipples. When Finnian told him to pinch them, he closed his eyes. *Put your other hand between your legs and touch your inner thighs. Slowly.* Corbin stoked the sensitive skin of his thigh and felt his cock harden against his stomach. He switched hands, pinching his nipples and sliding his palm along his other thigh. He imagined what it would be like for the hand to belong to a lover, for the touch to be unfamiliar.

The hand would be larger than his, rougher, and would rasp his delicate flesh until he trembled and pressed into it. He flexed his hips under the water, every nerve ending lit up at the thought.

Get out of the tub and dry off, but don't touch your erection. Go lie on the bed and light the candle. Then get the lube and wait for me.

Corbin sloshed water on the floor as he got out, but ignored it, roughly toweling himself off. Water dripped from his hair and ran down his spine like the lick of a tongue. The candle he lit filled the room with a subtle, warm scent. Amber and willow and musk. It was so tied to memories of pleasure that just the smell of it threw Corbin deeper into an erotic haze.

Lube in hand, he lay on the bed and waited.

I love to look at you. You're so beautiful, Corbin. You would do anything I asked you to, wouldn't you?

"Yes," Corbin gasped. "What do you want me to do?" His voice was rough and he squirmed against the duvet.

Finnian whispered in his ear and Corbin obeyed. He took out the vibrator with the wicked curve that hit his prostate. He slicked it with lube and lay back, teasing his hole with the tip. Finnian liked to tease.

Slick your fingers and open yourself up just a little. Just so I can see.

Corbin's touch was electric, and he slowly worked two fingertips around his rim and then inside himself, breathing deeply at the penetration and the feel of his own body on his fingertips.

His mind spiraled out as it always did when he took his time with this. He imagined his fingers grew into tree roots, long enough to slide all the way inside him, so deep they were buried in his gut, his heart, his lungs, the back of his throat. He imagined drawing a line of fiery pleasure from his ass to his throat, with strokes that opened his whole body. The openness he so often felt made real. His entire body penetrated, stuffed, all the empty places filled.

The image made him quake with lust, and he was hard and hot and throbbing. He moaned and Finnian's eyes heated.

Slide the vibrator inside, slowly, until the tip touches your prostate.

Corbin's eyes fluttered closed again as the toy breached him. His hips rolled up, the wet tip of his dick sliding against his stomach in a snap of pleasure.

Is it in place? Is it touching you just right?

Corbin flexed the toy and gasped, nodded.

Good. Hold it inside and take your hands away.

Corbin clenched around the toy and grabbed at his thighs. He scratched red lines in the pale flesh as his hips rocked, the tip of the toy crackling pleasure at the base of his spine.

Turn it on now, on low.

When the humming vibrations hit his prostate, Corbin's hips jerked upward and he cried out. Eyes closed to blackness, the warm scent of amber and musk making his head swim, he felt every sensation concentrate on that single spot inside his body. Every nerve ending routed there, stimulated with vibration, and Corbin gasped.

Touch yourself. Anywhere but your cock.

Corbin's concentration broke, easing things off a little. He ran his palm flat along his stomach, smearing drips of his arousal into his skin. He pinched his nipples, zinging pleasure to his gut. He slid a hand around his throat, felt his hard swallow.

He squeezed just enough to make himself writhe on the bed at the thought that it was all connected: blood and bone and come and spit and breath.

Turn it up a click and pulse it inside yourself. Do not touch your dick.

Corbin's breath came fast as the vibration increased. He rocked the vibrator, pulsing it against his prostate, lightheaded with jolts of pleasure that were turning his bones to liquid fire. He felt like he might drown in the sensation. The scratches on his thighs burned as he ran his fingernails the other way, and he knew he'd feel them the next day. Knew his jeans would rasp against the scratches and he'd remember this moment.

The pleasure, the pain, everything in between, it all tethered him inside his body, kept him in the world.

His hips had begun to move rhythmically, his entire body pulsing toward completion.

Turn it up the rest of the way. Fuck yourself. I want to watch you fall apart.

His groan was a broken thing clawing its way out of his throat. He turned up the vibration and his head snapped back as his body shook. He pushed the toy deep inside himself, and the thought was back. The image of pressing the thing all the way inside, dragging the shuddering pleasure up through the hollow of gut, the throb of heart, the gasp of lung, the clench of throat, the entirety of his body held captive to these sensations.

Only, for the first time, it wasn't the toy or his own fingers he pictured turning to tree roots or to fire. It was a lover's erection, and it speared through him, claiming him—all of him.

Corbin's back seized as every muscle clenched in throbbing pleasure, his cock shooting untouched onto his stomach and chest, a hot brand of lust. His muscles clenched around the toy, hips jerking as every touch to his prostate sent another jolt through him.

"Please," Corbin whimpered, shuddering as ecstasy turned to

pain. His cock gave one last pulse, a bead of come welling from the tip, and Finnian let him go.

You can turn it off now, if you like.

Fucked too loose for coordination, Corbin pulled the toy out and dropped it on the bed, collapsing backward. The still vibrating toy nudged his balls and he jerked again, a ghost spasm of pleasure turning to shivers. When he finally got ahold of it and turned it off, he was shaking.

He mopped at his stomach and then pulled the duvet over him, relaxing into the warmth. The candle would burn all night, and if he woke, its smell would remind him how good his body could feel. How good he could feel, even alone.

Always alone.

With a last sigh, he closed his eyes, but as he drifted to sleep, he realized it hadn't been an anonymous lover he'd pictured in the moment before his orgasm had ripped through him. It hadn't even been Finnian.

It had been Alex Barrow inside him. Inside him so deep he could never hope to get away.

WHEN CORBIN SAW Alex early the next morning, sleepy in the predawn light, he took in the muss of Alex's soft hair, the line of his broad shoulders, the movement of his throat as he swallowed.

Corbin saw these things and he squeezed his thighs together, the rough seam in the denim rasping over the scratches on his thighs. Corbin caught a whiff of Alex's scent and felt the press of his flesh against flesh, and he closed his eyes as his cock hardened in seconds. He closed his eyes and went elsewhere in his head, because he'd never been so close to coming from practically nothing in his life.

When Alex squeezed his arm in greeting, Corbin bit his lip and tried to smile, and he decided he would bake and bake and bake the curse away every night if he had to. Because he wanted Alex fucking Barrow. He wanted him like he'd never wanted anything.

Chapter Nine

IT WAS HAPPENING MORE and more often. Little touches at work, and Alex's smell in his nose, and when he got home, instead of Finnian telling him what to do, it was Alex.

Alex who stripped him bare. Alex who ran greedy eyes over his naked form. Alex who had him touch himself everywhere, fuck himself with every toy he owned, scream his orgasms into the empty quiet of the house and the yard and the woods beyond.

It was Alex, Alex, Alex, inside his head and inside his body, until he was so full up with Alex, it was like his fantasy had come true.

It wasn't just sex, either. Something about Alex *called* to him. He dreamt about him. He began imagining that Alex was sitting across from him at the kitchen table over dinner. Walking with him when he and Wolf tramped the honeycomb trails through the trees. More than that, he imagined Alex talking to him. He imagined talking to Alex.

Corbin had never talked to anyone—not really. His aunts had mostly talked at him when it was needed, preferring to talk to each other. Carbon, Lex, and Jasmine knew what he was thinking, so he never had to tell them. Finnian . . . Finnian wasn't much for talking. Which left Wolf. He told Wolf things sometimes. They felt like confessions, but he thought perhaps Wolf knew already in the same way Carbon, Lex, and Jasmine did.

But Alex didn't know, and Corbin thought that he might want to.

The afternoon before, as they'd cleaned up the kitchen, Corbin had been muttering to himself, and Alex asked "Will you tell me what you're talking about?" Flustered, Corbin's head had immediately emptied. He hadn't even realized it had been audible, and had raised his brows questioningly at Alex. "I want to know," Alex had murmured. "I want to know everything."

Corbin had snuck in to perform the ritual three more times since first doing it. Each time he stood in And Son's kitchen, hands dusty with flour and the scent of yeast in the air, he concentrated on pouring the curse into the challah. He imagined it drowned in egg, cut by salt, enrobed in flour, and anchored by braiding. Then he watched as the oven devoured it, not leaving until it was reduced to carbon.

And while he couldn't be certain—there was so little certainty with these things—he thought he felt . . . lighter. He felt like he had as a child, when the forces of the world were friends, and his navigation of them a kind of play. When he'd dipped in and out of flows of energy like they were rivers and he could see the terminus.

He felt . . . Was that happiness?

Still, he couldn't trust it. Couldn't trust Alex's very *life* to a maybe. He touched Alex cautiously, and watched intently, always on the lookout for signs that some hint of his poison had rubbed off. Alex seemed all right—but not unaffected. He seemed to feel the weight behind Corbin's touches, even if he couldn't know what it indicated.

One morning, Corbin woke early, full up with a sense of purpose. He showered quickly, then made his way to And Son in the predawn.

He felt a tugging at his skin, like he was being hurried along. The dark, chilly wind pressed him forward, leaves sweeping him onward, and shadows of branches laying an urgent path before him. His mouth tingled, the snap of sugar hot on his tongue.

All the signs pointed to the same thing. That it was time for the final ingredient. That, this morning, Corbin was going to reverse polarity. He was going to bake his positive feelings into the bread and give it to Alex. *Bake with love for those you love and they will taste the sweetness*. These things always cut both ways.

He'd decided to stick with challah—the braid seemed apt, and he'd felt the way the woven strands strengthened his intentions. As the yeast bubbled, he thought of the fizz he got in his stomach when Alex stood close to him, the warmth of his skin a tantalizing promise. As he mixed oil and egg with flour and salt, watching them bleed into each other, he imagined the ways he wanted his mind and Alex's to become one, their thoughts merging. As the dough rose, he pictured rising with Alex in the early morning, soft pillows and warm arms and hot breath. As he braided the dough, he pictured the way their bodies would entwine, edges obliterated as they sank into one being in a form more beautiful than either could make apart.

One piece of yourself to sign it, his aunts had always said, so Corbin pressed the lightest of kisses to the top of the risen braid before putting it in the oven. This time, he didn't want it to burn. This time, he wanted it to bake perfectly. For its scent to fill Alex's nose even before he consumed it.

The timer went off just as the door to the kitchen swung open, and Alex walked in.

"Corbin, hi. You're not scheduled today."

Corbin slid the challah from the oven but froze, still holding it, because someone else had come into the kitchen behind Alex. The air around the man was mottled and twisted with fear, pain, shame, and shot through with hope, determination, and relief.

He also had Alex spangled all over him. In his hair, clinging to his clothes, on his skin. And he stuck close to Alex like he didn't want more than a foot of space between them.

Corbin's gut clenched with a pain he'd never felt before. It was so different from what he'd felt when his aunts died, or his mother never came back, that it didn't feel like the same emotion.

Then, he'd felt adrift, his edges tattered and torn at by the wind. Now, he felt like something planted deep inside him, something nascent and delicate and yearning, had been crushed in a fist and torn out of him by the roots.

"Corbin?"

The pan clattered on the wooden countertop, and Alex slid it away from the edge and took his potholders.

The man with the aura like bruises looked at him intently. He was pale as milk and thin, like Corbin, though a few inches shorter. Delicate bones and haunted eyes the color of a blank summer sky. A puff of hair bleached as white as a dandelion seed head, the sides shaved aggressively short, with a line cut to the scalp.

This man was beautiful and sharp and vulnerable, and of course Alex would want him. Alex could have him.

Why would Alex want poison when he could have sustenance. Why would Alex choose an ankle-snapping trap when he could have a warm embrace. Corbin was broken and deadly and ruinous. This man, though worn around the edges, was potential and companionship and joy.

Corbin wanted to throw up.

Alex's hand closed around his shoulder, and his traitorous body relaxed automatically.

"Corbin. Are you with me?"

I'm always with you.

Corbin nodded, and forced himself to meet Alex's gaze. His eyes were warm and concerned, and Corbin's heart beat in the hollow of his throat, because in his dreams Alex looked at him that way just before he enfolded Corbin in his arms.

"This is Gareth, my friend from New York. Remember?"

My best friend got hurt. He's going to come stay with me for a while.

Corbin nodded again and gazed at the man—Gareth. The name didn't fit him. Gareth extended a hand and when Corbin took it, their eyes locked. They both felt the snap. Friends, then. Or at least not enemies. But Corbin felt something more, too. Gareth was like him. Just a little bit. It was long buried, disavowed, unacknowledged in the light of day. But Gareth had that spark in him, and Corbin could feel the way like called to like.

Gareth's clear blue eyes narrowed in unconscious recognition. He dropped Corbin's hand and gestured between himself and Alex. "We're friends, not lovers. We'll always be friends, not lovers. I mean, there was that one week when we first lived togeth — Uh, yeah, but we're not together."

Corbin felt like he could breathe again, and he knew he was blinking stupidly at Gareth but he couldn't stop.

Alex was shaking his head minutely, but he was on the edge of laughter.

"Anyway, I'm starving," Gareth said, throwing himself onto the counter and swinging his legs. "Is that edible?" He pointed at the challah.

Corbin realized he hadn't yet spoken when he tried to answer and found he couldn't. It happened sometimes—things on the inside swelling to stop the words from getting out. He opened his mouth to try again and felt the tiny seed of panic that always lived there. *What if my words never come back?*

Corbin pushed the challah toward Alex, since he couldn't speak.

"Is this for me?" Alex said slowly, his voice low. In moments like this one, Corbin knew that Alex *saw* him. Alex didn't have the spark. Alex was as earthy and present as a sapling, with roots that would deepen over time even as he grew into the sky. But he *felt* what Corbin was, what Corbin meant, what Corbin needed, in a way that made Corbin vibrate with rightness.

At Corbin's nod, Alex smiled. "Thank you." His pleasure was simple and warm. He leaned in to smell it and his smile widened. "Cinnamon and sugar challah? What a good idea." Corbin cocked his head because it wasn't quite right. "Cinnamon toast challah," Alex corrected himself, and Corbin's heart pounded *yes.*

"Okay, okay, I get it. It's for Alex." Gareth shot Alex an amused look. "But can I please have some too? Helen cooked last night, so obviously I didn't eat anything. I don't know how you survived growing up on that, much less ate enough to be all . . . football-y," he said to Alex.

"I didn't. My dad always cooked."

"Oh, right. Sorry," Gareth muttered, and tugged Alex's sleeve once in apology. But Alex waved it off.

Then they were both looking at Corbin, and he felt something new stir inside him, like a small thing with sheathed claws unfurling in his chest from hibernation. He did want to share the bread with Gareth. Gareth was important—was *going* to be important. He belonged here. He was part of the picture.

Corbin's voice was only a croak, but it must have sounded affirmative enough because Gareth practically dove at the challah. As Gareth's pale fingers tore a chunk from its side, Corbin felt the tug within him.

Yes, yes, yes, this is right.

Alex shot Gareth an irritated look, and Corbin could see his possessiveness. The braid was his and Gareth had damaged it. He cut a slice of his own, the air suddenly redolent with cinnamon, and Corbin's eyes were magnetized to Alex's mouth as he took a bite, chewed, swallowed.

Yes, yes, yes, yes.

Alex's eyes widened and Corbin knew he could taste it. He might not recognize it for what it was, but it didn't matter.

Bake with love for those you love and they will taste the sweetness.

"It's perfect," Alex said.

Gareth garbled something complimentary through a full mouth, but his gaze on Alex and Corbin was sharp and assessing. Gareth saw.

Alex cut another slice of challah and held it out to Corbin. "A baker should always taste his recipes."

Corbin chewed, the give of the challah just right between his teeth, the bloom of sugar on his tongue just right against the richness of the bread and the earthiness of cinnamon. It was the relief of rest after sleepless nights combined with the comfort of Alex's presence. When he swallowed, Corbin felt eased. Yes, it was right.

He got lost in the tangled web of associations inside his head, and came out of it to the touch of Alex's hand on his arm. And now he didn't have to take himself away from Alex's touch, did he?

"Did you know it's Thanksgiving?" Alex was saying, as if perhaps he were repeating himself. Corbin stared at him. He hadn't known. "I don't think we'll get that much business, but I thought we'd do a few simple things. Some bread, anyway." When Corbin's words still didn't come, Alex went on. "You're not on the schedule, but if you want to hang out, of course I always love your company."

He said it matter-of-factly, but a shade of hopeful energy was there in the air around him.

"Obviously, you're staying," Gareth said, jumping down from the counter and clapping him on the back. "Do you talk? It's cool if you don't, I just want to know whether I'm asking polite questions or torturing you. I only like to torture people on purpose." He leered, and Corbin blinked at him.

Finally, the words were there, the blockage cleared away.

Corbin turned to Alex. "You don't celebrate Thanksgiving."

"No, I don't. I don't want to close the bakery in honor of it, but I also don't want to make a bunch of stuff no one's going to buy. Usually, it's no big deal since we take it all to Food Gatherers." That was the local homeless shelter and meal service that And Son donated all their leftovers to. "But on Thanksgiving, they're actually inundated with donations, so it's not as helpful."

"Even though Alex doesn't celebrate horrible Thanksgiving, we're still going to hang out tonight after we close up, in a totally non-celebratory manner, because I've been cooped up in that damn house for over a week and I'm climbing the walls. And you're going to hang out with us."

Corbin could see how Gareth and Alex were such good friends. They were the inverse of one another, Alex's gentle geniality covering gut-deep confidence and iron will, Gareth's snappy bluster the veneer over a slightly nervous desire for approval.

For the next two hours, they baked companionably. Gareth, Alex explained, was a chef, so while he didn't have Alex's experience with baking, he could follow directions well enough to help with everything.

Once they opened, the day passed in stretches of down time broken by a few flurries of activity. They sold most of the bread and a lot of coffee to harried holidaymakers, and watched as a group of teenagers lingered over lattes, clearly attempting to avoid the inevitable moment when they had to leave the joy of each other's easy company and go home to family celebrations they dreaded.

Around four, Gareth went to the market down the street before it closed and came back with a bag of groceries for the dinner he said he was going to cook them.

Corbin had spent hours drawing, in the downtime between baking and cleaning. (He didn't interact with customers. He'd made that clear when Alex had hired him.) But rather than draw scenes with Carbon, Jasmine, Lex, and Finnian, Corbin found himself sketching Alex and Gareth. Not drawing them into his imaginings, not making up stories, but rendering them as they were—Alex's strong arms and broad shoulders bent toward kneading bread, a lock of hair falling over his forehead. Gareth's easy smiles and glittering eyes with the customers, and his tense expression when he thought no one was looking.

"Can I see?" Alex asked, pulling up a chair next to where Corbin was sitting. Corbin scraped his hair behind his ear and slowly flipped the notebook back two pages. "Wow." Alex searched his face. "I've only ever seen your more comic style stuff. These are incredible."

Corbin ducked his chin.

"I'm serious. You're really talented."

Corbin *hmm*ed but didn't know what to say. *Compliments are unnecessary and pandering*, his aunts had always insisted. *Either the* *person you're complimenting already knows, or they won't believe it anyway.*

"You about ready to take off? That is, you don't *have* to come hang out with us if you don't want to. But we're going to leave soon, if you do."

Corbin cleared his throat. He didn't even know what hanging out would mean. "Do you want me to."

"Yeah, of course I do. Absolutely," Alex said, squeezing Corbin's shoulder. Flushed and vibrating with satisfaction, Corbin nodded and gathered his things.

They made their way through the silence of downtown in Alex's car, Corbin watching out the window as the birds streaked overhead, three by three.

Gareth's voice startled him. "I'm seriously sick of the walls at your place, Alex. Corbin, do you live alone?"

"Yes."

"Can we go to your place instead?" Gareth spun around in his seat and batted his eyelashes. "Please? For real, I don't want to go back to Alex's."

"I— All right. It's just not very . . . I don't have people over," Corbin stammered.

"Well, do you have a kitchen?"

"Yes."

"Do you have a table and chairs—or a floor?"

"I— Yes, of course."

"Then great, let's go there."

"Gareth," Alex warned. "We weren't invited."

"He said 'all right'!"

"Corbin, we don't have to come over if you don't want."

Corbin remembered the day he brought Portia Washington home with him from the park. They'd been climbing on the monkey bars, then they'd drifted over to a hollow stump where they played potions, mixing dirt with crushed berries. Corbin had told Portia that his aunts had real potions, and she'd wanted to see, so they'd walked together, kicking at rocks and chunks of fallen wood.

When Aunt Jade had found them rummaging through their stores of dried herbs and unguents, she'd been furious, and Portia had run away, afraid of Aunt Jade's anger and the scar that twisted her mouth. The scar which Aunt Jade always said was the souvenir of a car accident, but which Corbin came to suspect later had a somewhat more sinister origin.

He'd never asked another person home. It hadn't helped that soon after, the other children at the park and the farmer's market had begun talking about the boy who lived in the haunted house, and the scary witches who lived there with him. When he'd told his aunts, they'd laughed and exchanged knowing glances. *It happens every ten years or so*, Aunt Hilda had told him. But Corbin had felt the pain underneath her flippant reply and wished he'd never mentioned it.

"No," he told Alex. "I want you to." *It's my house now*, he told himself. Of course it was. It had been for years, but this felt like a step toward feeling the truth of it.

When they stepped out of the car, Corbin saw the moon hanging heavy and nearly full in the sky, a thin cover of cloud turning the light milky and delicate. Then, as Alex walked toward the house, the cloud was blown away, moonlight falling on Alex like a consecration. He glowed with it, illumined against the dark angles of the house. It took Corbin's breath away.

"He thinks you aren't attracted to him. He's not even sure you notice him at all." Gareth's voice was pitched low, his words so absurd Corbin almost couldn't make sense of them.

Alex commanded his entire focus, as nothing ever had. He imagined he radiated it whenever he looked at Alex.

"I can tell you do, though. You do notice him. Right?"

Corbin stared at the ground, then nodded.

"Good. He deserves to be noticed."

Chapter Ten

GARETH'S BAG had revealed a bottle of whiskey in addition to the ingredients for dinner, and Gareth pushed it across the counter to Corbin and then waved both of them over to the table so they weren't in the way as he cooked.

"This place is wild," Gareth said as he took out pans, knives, and a cutting board. "Your parents must've been pretty into cooking with a kitchen this big?"

"My aunts."

"They raised you?"

"Yes. My father died before I was born, and my mother wasn't around."

"They cook a lot?"

"Sometimes." Corbin pictured the late-night or early-morning feasts, and the days on end of cheese sandwiches in between. "They liked to cook elaborate meals, but then they'd lose interest for a while. Or they'd leave a pot of chili on the fire and just add bits to it."

"On this?" Corbin nodded and Gareth examined the round-bottomed pot that hung over the grate in the fireplace. "Wow. I love it. Very double double, toil and trouble. There weren't three of them were there?"

Alex shook his head, but he was smiling.

"No, two," Corbin said. He eyed the bottle on the table, and Alex, following his gaze, raised an eyebrow.

"Want one?"

"I don't know."

"Do you like whiskey?"

"I don't know."

"Okay, let's try." Alex poured a splash into one glass and handed it to Corbin, their fingers brushing softly, then poured a more sizable amount into his own glass. "Cheers," Alex said, clinking them together. The tinkling of the glasses touching rang out, clear as a bell in the cavernous kitchen.

Maybe this is what friends do.

Corbin sniffed and the scent reached up his nose with thick fingers. It took him back to curling in bed as a child, lungs rattling and skin dry and hot.

"I think my aunts used to put this in my cough medicine."

Gareth and Alex laughed, but Corbin could recall the sluggish feeling he got after drinking the cordial, crawling under the covers and sleeping for hours. It made him miss his aunts with a sudden pang he hadn't felt in years.

He sipped the amber liquid and felt the burn reach down his throat as well as up the back of his nose. It tasted like heat and plants and fire. When he slid his glass back across the table for more, Alex grinned at him.

When he'd finished his drink, Corbin sensed Wolf was near. He stumbled against the edge of the table and Alex's arm shot out and caught him. Gareth snorted from the stove, but Corbin didn't care. For once, he felt warm and floaty, in alignment with the flows of energy. Alex's hand on his hip lingered there a moment and Corbin felt it through jeans and sweater, felt its loss as he moved toward the door.

Winter was a promise in the air, and Corbin shivered in his wool sweater. Wolf tramped toward him, Stick close behind.

"Where's everyone else." Corbin scratched both dogs' ears.

In the woods, in the woods, in the woods.

"You coming inside tonight." Wolf tipped his head, considering the question, then puffed up his fur and settled in on his haunches next to the door. Not tonight, then, but soon. Corbin knelt and threw his arms around Wolf's neck, burying his face in fur. "Night."

They went inside, and Corbin fed Stick. The smells of bacon, butter, and parsley filled his nose as the warmth of the kitchen welcomed him.

"Corbin," Alex said, catching his elbow. "Aren't you cold?" He gestured to the knees of Corbin's jeans, which were wet from where he'd knelt in the snow.

"I'll make a fire," Corbin said.

"Why don't you change out of those pants?" Alex asked. Gareth snorted again.

"Oh, right. Okay." Corbin shivered as he walked upstairs. The subtle command in Alex's voice had put Corbin in mind of all the things he'd imagined Alex commanding him to do. In his bedroom, he fumbled out of his wet jeans and into dry corduroys, but the air was humming and there was a buzzing in his ears that usually meant something was about to happen.

Downstairs, he built a fire in the living room fireplace and then rejoined Alex and Gareth in the kitchen. Alex's eyes lingered on his pants in a way that made Corbin flush.

"Sorry," Alex said. "I guess I was just expecting sweats or pajamas or something."

"I don't have any." Corbin always slept naked, loving the sensuous slide of sheets and blankets against his limbs in the winter, the cool breeze raising hairs on his arms and legs in the spring and autumn, and the warm sun falling on his bare skin on summer mornings. Alex's eyes heated and he gulped the rest of his whiskey, looking away.

Corbin slid back into his seat and filled his own glass. After a minute, Alex and Gareth started talking easily, and he lost himself in the ebb and flow of their words. When Gareth put something in the oven, then pulled out the chair across from him, Corbin wasn't sure how much time had passed.

"Okay, so no bullshit about what we're thankful for. Let's play Never Have I Ever instead."

"Are you thirteen?" Alex asked.

"Never Have I Ever is a drinking game, so I did *not* play it when I was thirteen. Besides, it's a great way to get to know each other," Gareth insisted, looking pointedly at Corbin.

"I don't know that game." Corbin wasn't much for games.

"It's easy. You say 'Never Have I Ever,' and then fill in the blank. Anyone who has done the thing has to drink."

"Why," Corbin said, and Alex started laughing.

"No reason. Just for fun," Gareth said. Corbin wrinkled up his nose, confused. "Okay, how about . . . Either Or?" Gareth offered.

"Or we could just talk like adults," Alex said.

"*Some* of us don't seem to talk that much," Gareth said. Corbin knew it was him.

"Well, that's all right," said Alex.

"Listen, Corbin. Are you cool with playing a few rounds of Either Or? I say two things and you pick one. Feel free to explain your answer. Easy."

"Pick one to do what."

Gareth narrowed his eyes. "Here, we'll demonstrate. Alex, lakes or oceans?"

"Lakes. The ocean is exciting and dramatic, but a lake is steady, predictable."

"See?" Gareth asked.

"So it's which you like more," Corbin tried.

"Sometimes. Or which you identify more with, or which excites you more, et cetera. Here, Alex, ask me."

Alex sighed long-sufferingly. "All right. Gareth, ketchup or mustard?"

"You're a bastard and you know I hate that question. Fine, mustard. Because ketchup is delicious on fries, but mustard has many uses and is the base of great vinaigrettes and so I have to choose mustard, damn you."

Corbin had the distinct sense he was missing something, but he nodded.

"Great! Okay, Corbin, hmm . . . Oh, calm down, Alex. I swear, I have *no* idea what he thinks I'm going to ask you!" Gareth snickered. "Okay, uh, fate or free will?"

Corbin choked on his drink, throat closing around fire. Through a strangled cough, Alex swam in front of his eyes. Alex, in his aunts' kitchen. Alex, where no other man had ever been. Alex looking at him like he might want to stay there.

Fate wasn't a word the aunts ever used. It was too crude, too blunt an instrument to describe the delicate play of energy streams that intertwined like a symphony in the universe. There were things you couldn't control—things so vast, composed of so many moving parts, so sunk into the fabric of the world, that to untangle them would be the work of more than one lifetime.

This was the curse. A brand that marked the Wales—not because of inevitability, but because of the way heat cut an imprint into wood or flesh. The result of a brand wasn't fate; it was the laws of nature. Still, both were unchangeable without the ability to unwrite what nature had written.

But no matter how complex the things you couldn't control, there were always ways to shift the flow. Ways to read the signs, to see how the universe was nudging you, and choose to obey or not. If you were attuned to them, they could give you a sense of what was coming, an idea where to go. Obeying made life easier, helped you follow the path that would be advantageous. The Wales were attuned. The Wales were very attuned.

It was a balance. If you were cursed, it was only fair to give you instruments to divine it.

But lately, Corbin had begun to feel that perhaps things were shifting, inverting. That, perhaps, his sense of which were the beads and which the thread was backward. Because Alex felt like an energy stream all his own—one strong enough that he was exerting a force on everything else in Corbin's life.

Corbin had thought Alex was a sign pointing at the curse. But what if all the signs were pointing to Alex?

It crumpled Corbin's mind like a page torn from a notebook, pieces touching unexpectedly, wrinkles making all new lines. Could a leaf be torn from the world as easily? Reformed with as little as a squeeze of the hand? If what Corbin had always known to be unchangeable was shifting, what solid ground did he have? Had his aunts known? Had they seen signs of their own?

Questions piled on questions until Corbin's vision started to flip into his inside world instead of what was before him.

"Corbin. Corbin, hey." Strong hands reached for him and a soft voice pulled him right-side out again. Alex.

He blinked, vision confused, and heard someone whimper. For a moment he worried it was him, but then he realized that Stick had nosed between his knees and he was clutching her fur in sweat-dampened fists. She whined as he let go and rested her chin on his knee until he laid a gentle palm back on her head.

"I'm sorry," Gareth said softly. "Let's not play this game anymore. I'm an idiot. I was just trying to break the ice and get you to talk. Sorry. Shit, sorry, Corbin."

Alex left one hand on Corbin's shoulder and laid the other on Gareth's arm, shaking his head. In that moment, Corbin saw so clearly who Alex was. The man whose touch could gentle. The man whose presence soothed. The man who was so full up with weighty presence he had ballast to spare.

His aunts had had a name for people like Alex. *Kedge*. The mooring that kept things from drifting off, kept them anchored to the here and now.

Gareth stood and pulled a pan from the oven. While he put together a salad, Corbin and Alex sat in silence, eyes meeting and parting, Stick sitting between them. The room drifted in and out of focus, and Corbin found words welling up in his throat. The wind outside whistled plaintively through the wind chimes and shook the words loose.

"This is the first time anyone's been in this house since my aunts. Except the time you came in to use the bathroom," he added. "First time anyone cooked who wasn't them or me." He shook his head in surprise. His lips felt a little numb. "'S nice not to be alone for a little while."

He immediately felt disloyal to Carbon and Lex, Jasmine and

Finnian, who'd kept him from being completely alone. But he thought they'd know what he meant.

Alex encouraged Stick to move, then yanked Corbin's chair close so they were facing each other. He put his hands on Corbin's shoulders and looked into his eyes.

"You don't have to be alone anymore. Not if you don't want to be."

The sincerity in his gaze shook something dangerous loose in Corbin's stomach and he blinked away tears. Alex didn't know—couldn't know—the torment his promise induced.

Corbin breathed through it. He didn't think he could put Alex in danger by taking him up on all that the offer implied. Not unless he was absolutely sure he had bled the curse out of himself. Baked it out. And even though he'd sensed a shift, you could never be sure with these things.

Even now, when he could feel the warmth of Alex's hands through his sweater, he found himself afraid of reaching out to him, afraid to touch him—the darkness he had so long known he could transmit still lay between them, in Corbin's fear, if nowhere else. But his skin was awakened to Alex's touch, buzzing like it wanted to lift off Corbin's weighty bones and seek a greener pasture.

A pan *thunk*ed onto the table and a bowl of salad followed.

"Bacon and new potato frittata with chèvre, smoked paprika, and a parsley sauce. Baby greens with roasted garlic and lemon oil dressing, and parmesan croutons."

"Looks beautiful," said Alex.

"Thank you," Corbin said, awed. He didn't know what a frittata was, but it appeared to be eggs. Eggs, bacon, and potatoes couldn't be bad. His aunts had never told him what he was eating. The food smelled amazing, but Corbin's head spun when he moved to fill his plate.

"Whoa, lightweight, I got it," Gareth said, and dished him a perfect slice of frittata and a green burst of salad that looked like spring and smelled like summer.

Gareth and Alex talked and joked as they ate. The food was delicious and Corbin felt better after he'd eaten, less floaty. Sometimes when he forgot to eat, his sense of smell grew more acute. But even with a full stomach, he could smell the way his familiar house took on the scents of the evening. Bacon and lemon, garlic and cheese, parsley and whiskey and companionship. And a light scent the color of green apple or the underside of a leaf turned toward the coming rain. Possibility.

After they ate, Gareth demanded a tour of the house. "This place is like Thornfield Hall," he muttered.

Corbin trailed behind them as they walked through his home. His aunts' home. Seeing it through unfamiliar eyes, it was clear he only lived in a third of the house, while the rest possessed the undisturbed stillness of an altar or a grave.

The tastes of whiskey and bacon were heavy on his tongue, but when Gareth pushed open the heavy door of Aunt Jade's bedroom, all Corbin could taste was lilac. He must have made a sound because Alex shut the door and herded them back downstairs into the living room in front of the fire.

"What happened to them?" Gareth asked softly.

Corbin swallowed another mouthful of whiskey and stared into the fire, tongues of flame joining and tearing themselves apart again.

"They died. When I was fifteen." He lay down on his back on the worn rug, eyes on the fire so he couldn't see Alex or Gareth. "I got home from school one day and they were the same as always. I stayed in my room most of the next couple of days. It must've been the weekend, I guess. I got hungry so I came downstairs and they weren't here."

The aunts only left the house upon rare occasions, preferring to send him to get whatever provisions they couldn't grow or make themselves.

"I knocked on Aunt Jade's door first but she didn't answer. Then Aunt Hilda's. I hadn't . . ."

He hadn't noticed any signs. Hadn't seen or heard or smelled anything out of phase. Hadn't tasted bitterness at the back of his tongue or felt the pricking of unease on the back of his neck. Their end had been hidden from him.

"I opened the door to Hilda's room and they were there. On the bed. Just . . . not there anymore."

The *nothingness* that had possessed the room when he'd opened the door had felt like a dream of falling where you never hit bottom. Measuring the ever-expanding emptiness with the length of your own body. His aunts were gone, and what they'd left behind wasn't the absence of them. It was the removal of everything they'd touched. Everything they'd influenced.

It was a crushing, begging, pawing nothingness that drove Corbin to his knees.

A nothingness that said: *This is where you start from now. This is how things are. Alone. Alone, alone, alone forever.*

"How did they die?" Gareth asked. Corbin heard what might have been Alex shoving Gareth.

"They died. They just died, it doesn't matter how."

But they'd died together, Corbin had comforted himself later. Then comfort had turned to fear when he'd realized he wouldn't have even that.

Alex didn't say anything for a while, but Corbin could feel his regard.

"Is that why you didn't come back to school?" he asked softly. "There were rumors, I remember."

"I forgot to go for a while," Corbin said simply.

Weeks, months, bleeding together like moments inside a chrysalis until Corbin had no choice but to emerge and see the world, a changed thing.

His head swam when he sat up. He'd never spoken of this with anyone. But the air was oil thick and the leaves outside the windows were limned in moonlight and Corbin felt reckless, intoxicated by the release of confession.

"I stayed with them for a little while," he said softly. "I didn't want to be alone."

He had curled up on the end of the bed like a cat, and stayed there for two days. What had made them the aunts wasn't there anymore, but it was something. A focal point, at least, so that the world didn't spin off its axis.

He'd made himself as small as he could, hugged his knees tight to his chest, and he'd stayed there with them, his only family, the only people who knew about him, about any of it. He'd stayed there and tried to forget that he couldn't keep them forever. That soon they'd be gone and he would be alone, truly alone. A speck of dust, wheeling through the infinite universe.

Corbin risked a glance at Alex and saw understanding in face. Yes, Alex *knew* things about him. He knew things that he didn't understand he knew.

Alex said Corbin's name silently, the shape of his mouth forming the word that held Corbin in place. Gareth had made himself invisible. Gareth saw in a different way.

The tension in the air sizzled. Alex held out a hand and Corbin took it, and the tension snapped like a shock wave. Gareth jumped to his feet and said, "Do you have any music here? We need music."

Corbin pointed and Gareth rummaged around in the cabinet, and put on one of the aunts' records. Corbin recognized it, could remember it playing when he was small, but couldn't have named it, and he sat with his eyes closed as the air lightened.

Gareth tugged him to his feet with the command to dance, and for the space of the next few songs, moments were detached, strobing. Corbin moved to the music, they laughed, and Stick ran around the living room, so joyful with the festive mood she almost bounced.

When Gareth went to the bathroom, he left Corbin and Alex standing there, inches apart. Whether Alex caught Corbin's arm, or Corbin turned to face him, he couldn't be sure. Every blink seemed to take eternity and Corbin couldn't break eye contact, saw only Alex, the rest of the world an indistinct swirl behind him.

They moved closer, closer, looking into each other's eyes. So close the air between them sparked and hummed. Corbin's mind flooded with the images of Alex he'd entertained while he was alone. In those, Alex would pull him flush against his body, kiss him roughly, tongue him open until he was panting.

In this reality, they breathed together, chests nearly touching on their inhalations, lips slightly parted like they could taste the sweetness of each other's air.

They stood, and the promise of a kiss formed between them, deferred.

Part Three ❧ Air

Alex

Chapter Eleven

"DUDE."

Gareth tried to tug Alex's arm away from his eyes, and Alex groaned and pulled away, rolling to face the back of the sofa where he'd collapsed the night before when they'd gotten home from Corbin's house.

Gareth gave up on his arm and flopped down to sit on his feet. "Dude."

"Since when do you say 'dude'?" Talking made his head throb worse.

"Since I need an introductory word that I can imbue with equal parts rebuke, awe, and casual interest. Which requires a long vowel and a slangy cultural context. You want to talk about it some more?"

"Just say whatever you're going to say and then leave me to die in peace."

At the word *die*, Alex was flooded with memories of the look on Corbin's face when he'd described his aunts' deaths. A kind of blank confusion, even all these years later.

"As I was going to say: *Dude*, he *really* likes you. Staring at you constantly like you might disappear at any moment, smelling you when you get close, always arranging himself so he's facing you, *likes* you. Plus he made you a challah and you both wanted to murder me for eating it."

"Was rude," Alex muttered, but he pulled himself to sit up because, while Gareth was occasionally very irritating—especially when feeling unconfident as he currently did—he was also the most socially astute observer of people that Alex had ever known.

Gareth smirked at him, recognizing that his bait had been taken.

"You think so?" Alex said. "Sometimes he's just so remote, and I can't tell if he's even paying attention."

"Well, do I think he's a complete weirdo? Without a doubt. But that doesn't mean he isn't also pretty deeply into you."

"Don't call him that."

Gareth's eyes widened and his mouth quirked up. "I'm sorry." He shook his head and shot Alex an eyebrow raise. "Wow. Okay, then."

They sat in silence for a while. Gareth flipped on the television to the Food Channel, where it now stayed. "Listen, I'm gonna take off for a while. Go camping. I miss it, and it'll be good timing. Why don't you invite him over? Try out some of those Chanukah recipes you want to use for the shop over the holidays. Just, bring him here instead of only awkwardly hanging out at And Son, okay? Christ, I hate that stupid name," he muttered.

He bit at his thumbnail, a strange expression coming over his face.

"And for the love of god, don't go back to that house until you're ready to fuck the kid within an inch of his life, because I swear there's something going on there."

"Going on? Care to elaborate?"

"No. Just, the vibe is all . . . something, I don't know. Not bad, just really tense. Didn't you feel it? Like we were being watched?"

"Nope. I was drunk. And distracted."

"No kidding. I'll leave in a couple days. No way I'm trying to buy gear today because everything will be swamped in the aftermath of your favorite holiday."

Alex made a face, but was too hungover to properly express his disgust at people celebrating Thanksgiving. Gareth had heard it all before, anyway.

ALEX ALMOST DIDN'T HEAR Corbin's knock, and smiled as he made his way to the door, because of course Corbin would knock instead of ringing the bell.

There was snow in his crow-black hair, like a dusting of sugar, and Alex drew him inside.

He hung Corbin's coat and said, "C'mere," leading him to the kitchen and drying off his hair with a clean tea towel. The dampness clumped Corbin's hair together like one of the comic book characters from Alex's youth. He was wearing ugly brown corduroys with sprung knees and another wool sweater, this one navy and cream, with unraveling cuffs, and Alex was flooded with fondness for him.

As Alex made tea, Corbin shifted his weight from foot to foot.

"Where's Gareth." His voice was cautious.

"He's camping. Up near Saginaw Bay."

Corbin cocked his head, his version of a question. "It's cold."

"Yeah, but Gareth's from Vermont. When he was a kid, he and his brothers would go winter camping, snowshoeing, cross-country skiing. His dad was big on that whole outdoorsy self-sufficiency. I know he hated it as a kid, but it was one of the first things we realized we had in common in New York. How both of us missed being able to just take off and be in nature. Nature without a view of skyscrapers, that is."

"New York City." Corbin spoke like he was tasting the words. "I don't think I would like it there. That's a lot of people. A lot of . . . stimulation."

"It is. I loved it some days. That feeling of excitement, in the air—almost magic. It was like anything could happen."

Corbin's eyes were sharp. "Magic," he whispered.

Alex poured them both tea and smiled.

"It felt that way. But the flip side of the magic was all that damn static. What felt like fun and possibility could also feel oppressive. Everything was so hard there, from getting around to buying groceries."

Corbin sipped his tea, nodding. "Things are . . . really hard sometimes. Just regular things. Here too, they're hard."

If that was true, and Alex was sure it was, Corbin was right that he wouldn't like New York. Wouldn't like the lack of fresh air to soothe his senses, or being bumped walking down the street, jostled on the subway.

"I never quite fit in with people there. Especially people who'd grown up in the city. It was all normal to them, and they didn't want to spend hours getting out of the city with me to go hiking or fish on a lake. We'd walk through a park, or go to the botanical gardens and they'd say, 'Here, some nature for you.' But it wasn't the same."

"I've never lived anywhere but here. Never been anywhere but here."

"Do you want to?" Alex studied Corbin's face, so much more expressive than his voice. He was gazing into his tea, but his eyes were sharp and present.

"No. Not really. I don't need to go somewhere different. I can make here be different any time I want."

"By imagining it?"

Corbin's gaze snapped to his like Alex had seen something he wasn't supposed to. Then Corbin relaxed and gave a one-shouldered shrug. "Yeah."

"You have an amazing imagination," Alex said. He wondered if it extended beyond the pages of Corbin's notebook, and the sudden flush of Corbin's cheeks told him that it did.

What would it be like, to dance with that imagination without barriers, without walls?

At Corbin's clear discomfort, Alex forced himself to take a step backward and a deep breath.

"So, I want to do Chanukah specials at the bakery. Some traditional things, like sufganiyot, but I also want to experiment. I want things people will get excited about. You want to help?"

Corbin nodded. "But I don't know what that is. And I don't really know anything about Chanukah."

"No problem. Sufganiyot are doughnuts. Jelly-filled doughnuts. But we could do some interesting flavors. I want to do a babka—that's a sweet yeast loaf filled with chocolate or cinnamon that you twist around and bake in a loaf pan so you can see all the lines of filling when you cut into it. I also like the idea of doing some sweet/savory and savory things. Have you had kugel?"

Corbin shook his head and Alex, thinking back to the kitchen and Corbin's description of the irregularly balanced meals of his childhood, imagined he hadn't tried a lot of things.

Alex wanted to make them all for him.

"Kugel is a casserole made with egg noodles and a mix of sour cream and cottage cheese and butter. It's lightly sweetened with sugar, or sometimes raisins, but it's not dessert sweet. It bakes up like a lasagna and you cut it into squares. But I thought we could do miniature kugels in muffin cups."

Corbin bit his lip. "That doesn't sound . . . very good."

Alex grinned. "I'll make it for you and you can see. But I think people will be into it. Your choice, then. Do you want to make kugel tonight, or sufganiyot?"

"Sufganiyot," Corbin said immediately.

"Okay, but I'm going to get you to try kugel eventually," Alex threatened.

Alex showed Corbin how to make the yeasted dough, and when they put it aside to rise, they sat in the living room.

"Do you celebrate the holidays?" Alex asked.

"No. My aunts celebrated the solstices, but not Christmas. Or Chanukah. I should know about it, but I don't."

"Do you want me to tell you?"

Corbin nodded, and drew his knees up, settling in like he wanted a story.

"Over two thousand year ago, Israel was ruled by Antiochus, the king of Syria. He wanted to unify his kingdom through a shared religion, so he suppressed Jewish traditions, outlawed rituals, and subjected elders of the temples to great dishonor. One respected rabbi was told he must eat pork, going against his Jewish dietary laws. He refused and was put to death. Soon, the fighting began, with small Jewish factions rising up to destroy the altars that were being built in the ashes of their temples."

Corbin's eyes were wide and intent. When Alex paused, he nodded for him to go on.

"One small group, called the Maccabees, was seen as particularly threatening, and Antiochus sent an expedition to destroy them. The Maccabees defeated the expedition, so the king sent another, which they also defeated. Finally, he sent an army of more than forty thousand. After many battles, the Maccabees defeated them as well, and went on to liberate Jerusalem. They entered the temple and swept away all the idols that vandals had left there, and built a new altar.

"The temple's golden menorah had been stolen, so they made another one, from whatever metal they could find. When they went to light the menorah, though, they only found one small jug of olive oil that had been blessed. It was only enough to light the menorah for one day."

Alex paused and Corbin leaned in.

"But, by a miracle, the oil burned for eight days, until more oil could be found. That's why we celebrate Chanukah for eight days, and why traditional Chanukah foods are cooked in oil. To celebrate the miracle that confirmed the Jews' right to practice their religion and keep their traditions despite the attempt to stamp them out."

Corbin's eyes had widened at mention of the miracle.

"That's the story. We celebrate Chanukah starting on the day of the rededication of the temple. It's on the Jewish calendar, though, so that's why it's a different time every year. It's also called the Festival of Lights, and my mom always said that she liked celebrating the idea that when they were cleaning up the vandalized temple by the light of the menorah, people were so joyous to be allowed to connect with their god again that it was a celebration. That joy has the power to do remarkable things. Joy can drive out the darkness. Even though we were never religious, she and my dad had a Chanukah party every year because they wanted to celebrate joy. Celebrate the way we can come together and be more powerful than the things that threaten us."

Alex remembered the smells and sounds of those parties, the house overheated from cooking and light and the press of bodies. The tang of oil and potato in the air, the endless games of dreidel, the whisper of snow from the windows thrown open against the heat the guests had created.

His mom had stopped throwing them after his dad died. The last one was the day after Alex came out to his parents. It had seemed a good time. Home from college for winter break, smitten with his first boyfriend, and enough removed from high school not to feel attached anymore to the person he'd been then.

His mom had grinned—he suspected she'd had an inkling already—and his dad had cried happy tears that he'd felt he could tell them. And maybe a few less happy ones that it had taken him years. They'd hugged him and smothered him in questions, and he'd gotten grumpy about answering them all and left to go for a walk, but the next morning they'd still been smiling when he came downstairs for breakfast.

He thought of that moment whenever he smelled latkes, the oil from the party that night mingling in his memory with his father's happy smile and his mother's twinkling eyes when she asked for details about his boyfriend.

"A miracle," Corbin murmured now, eyes fixed on a spot over Alex's head.

"Well. If you believe in that sort of thing. Call it a metaphor for faith, if you like. Okay, should we make some doughnuts?"

Alex reached out a hand and when Corbin took it automatically, he pulled the smaller man to his feet. A look of confusion crossed Corbin's face, and he took his hand away like he couldn't quite understand how it had gotten in Alex's.

They cut out circles of dough and covered them to rest again.

"Do you have a party now?"

"Hmm? Oh, a Chanukah party. No, I never have. When I moved to New York, I was dating this guy who loved Christmas. He loved the tree and the music and the parties, and I liked celebrating with him. It was nice to get swept up in everything. Chanukah . . . most people don't even think about it unless they're Jewish, so it tends to disappear. It was easier for a little while to just go with the Christmas flow."

Corbin pushed his hair back, leaving a streak of flour in the black strands, and it tugged at something in Alex's stomach.

"Also, I think . . . after my dad died, Chanukah didn't seem as festive. I didn't want to have my own Chanukah parties when I knew he wouldn't be there to fry the latkes, or to wrap all the presents in newspaper. He always picked relevant stories for each present."

Alex smiled to remember the year he was fourteen and he first realized that his father's thoughtfulness actually meant that it was pretty easy to guess what would be inside the wrapping. He'd never told his father that the big "surprise" of a box full of dozens of comics and graphic novels he'd asked for had revealed itself by being wrapped in the comics section of the newspaper.

"But after a few years—and after George and I broke up—I got kind of sad that Chanukah was this thing that I didn't do anything about. So I started getting together with friends intentionally. Not parties, just a dinner or a brunch. Sometimes we'd play dreidel as a drinking game." At Corbin's blank expression, Alex explained, "Dreidel. It's a game with a spinning top. I wanted Chanukah to feel cozy and be about togetherness. I wanted it to have that magic that Christmas has automatically. That's why it's important to me to have Chanukah pastries at the bakery."

Alex poured oil into a pot on the stovetop and clipped a thermometer to the side.

"Why did you break up."

"George and I?" George, with his white-blond hair and his

need for everything to be beautiful, had eventually come to seem more a work of art than a person. "We didn't have that much in common. So after a while, it just kind of fizzled out. He cared so much about how things looked that he sometimes forgot it was also about what they meant. He was a sweet, kind person, but we weren't right for each other."

"How do you know if someone's right."

There was a faint line between Corbin's dark brows, and Alex risked a step toward him.

"You just know, Corbin." Then shook his head at himself. "At least, I assume so. I don't think I've ever been with the right person."

Corbin seemed to be struggling with something. "But," he said sharply. "But *how*. How would you tell."

"Well. I think for me I would tell because I would feel comfortable around them after a while, as if I could be myself and they would like me for it. I would think of them first when I wanted to tell someone things that happened. If I were doing something or seeing something amazing and they weren't there, I would know that it would be better with their presence. I'd want to know everything about them. Even the bad stuff. And I would stand behind them, support them, feel proud that they had chosen me to spend their time with, to trust."

Alex trailed off, realizing he'd stepped even closer to Corbin.

"And you never felt those things. With those other men."

Alex shook his head. "No. It was all pale, a shadow of what I think it would feel like. They all wanted me, and I wanted them. But . . ." He ran his fingers through Corbin's hair, dusting the ground with flour. "They didn't *need* me. I didn't need them."

Corbin made a choked sound and squeezed his eyes shut. Alex's heart was pounding with the desire to crush them together, chest to chest, and hold on fiercely.

But Corbin looked pained. He clasped his hands together like one hand was keeping the other from reaching out, and a muscle jumped in his jaw.

Alex took a deep breath and cleared his throat, his blood like fire and his head light with desire.

He made himself move away from Corbin, and dropped three circles of dough into the oil. "You want to let them come just to golden brown and then flip them."

He bobbed the dough over in the oil, then scooped out the doughnuts when they'd browned and slid them onto a plate lined with paper towel.

"Here, you try." He handed Corbin the spider.

Corbin's hand trembled as he took the implement and stepped up to the stove. He flipped the doughnuts, let them brown, and removed them. Then he added more, and did it again. In a few minutes it was like he'd forgotten Alex was even there.

Then, on the last batch, he seemed to get lost somewhere between his mind and his hand. The spider hovered over the hot oil, but Corbin's eyes had drifted up and to the side, and Alex watched as the doughnuts turned from golden to brown to black.

Alex snaked a hand in front of Corbin and switched the stovetop off.

"Corbin," he said softly, and watched as his attention returned.

"I burned them. Sorry."

"Don't worry about it; we have plenty to experiment with."

"I don't always . . . I'm not the best with time. It goes such different speeds sometimes."

Alex nodded. He'd seen the moments when Corbin's attention caught on something and he rolled inside himself, the way Alex might lose himself watching a movie or reading a book. He'd also seen the moments when Corbin observed every detail with each of his senses, so present and attentive that it would seem as though time had slowed.

Alex was coming to love the way Corbin described how things felt, instead of how they were.

"What were you thinking about?"

"The oil. The . . . miracle. It was like a blessing. A way for their god to say they were getting it right. A sign. The oil was a sign."

Alex nodded, studying Corbin's expression. He looked hopeful, purposeful.

"That's the story, yeah. Do you believe in god?"

Corbin blinked slowly. His eyes were fathomless, the brown almost as dark as his pupils. "I believe in everything."

Chapter Twelve

FOR THE FOURTH night in a row, since he'd gotten back from camping, Gareth cooked as if he was back working in a restaurant.

"What the hell happened on that camping trip?" Alex said, as Gareth served him Moroccan chicken tagine with green olives and preserved lemons, coconut rice pilaf, stewed eggplant with yogurt and sesame oil, and a salad of watercress and frisée with poached quail's eggs.

Gareth looked different. The tightness around his eyes, as if he was always waiting for something to jump out at him, had eased, but in its place was a haunted hopelessness that made Alex nervous.

Gareth put both elbows on the table and rested his chin in his hands. "Did you know that I had a crush on you? After we slept together?"

Chicken caught in Alex's throat and he coughed spasmodically. "What?"

Gareth waved him away. "Don't hurt yourself. Just for a week or so, right after. I knew it'd never turn into anything. We were great as friends, and I knew there was no way we'd be good together, but just for a little while, I couldn't help but see you differently."

Alex stared. They'd slept together after a boisterous night out with friends, drunk on cheap vodka and the joy of companionship in the city. It had been fun and a little hot, with a lot of laughter and a clear sense of incompatibility. And Gareth had been the one, after, who had playfully bumped Alex's shoulder and said, "Don't be getting any ideas, Barrow. We're friends, okay?" before going back to his own room to sleep.

Alex had never felt anything romantic for Gareth, but he felt a *lot* for him. He was the best friend Alex had ever had—almost what he imagined a brother would be like. He felt protective of Gareth and invested in his happiness. The idea that he could have missed something so important was gutting.

"I—what—when did—"

"Seriously, shut it down, Alex. It's what I do, okay, and then it was done. Four days, five tops. Like a zillion years ago. Eat your food."

Alex ate because he didn't know what to say. It was delicious, as Gareth's food always was. Bold and delicate, balanced and interesting.

"I'm telling you because I was thinking about you when I was camping. You're like a cast-iron skillet. Incredibly strong and capable of withstanding high heat. Heavy, if someone's not used to it. And, if properly cared for, things that shouldn't don't stick. You don't even need to be washed, just wiped a little." Gareth's gaze was steady, assessing.

"Were you . . . playing a game called Which Kitchen Implement Are Your Friends or something?"

"No, I was playing a game called Why None of Alex Barrow's Lovers Ever Stick. You're handsome, charismatic, confident. You treat people with respect. You're genuinely interested and caring. You listen. You're occasionally even a little funny."

"Way to bury the barb, asshole."

"Look, not everyone's a comedian, you'll live. The point is, they don't stick because you keep yourself nicely seasoned and oiled and on the back burner ready for anything. And completely self-sufficient. You don't need anyone or anything. Not in a creepy, egomaniacal, broken way," he said quickly. "You're just . . . a closed system."

"Leaving aside for the moment the implicit scorn in what you just said, I actually told Corbin something pretty similar the other day."

"Do tell."

"We were making sufganiyot and he asked why it didn't work out with anyone I'd dated."

Gareth's eyes got big and he leaned in. "He's so *into* you, Jesus. Okay, sorry."

"I said that with everyone I've ever been with, we wanted each other, but we didn't need each other. You're saying I didn't need them because I'm a pan and, yeah, that's true. But *they* didn't need me, man. I was with Timo for four years, and he didn't *need* me. I hadn't really thought about it until I was standing there, looking at Corbin, and he—" Alex shook his head.

"He needs you."

Alex shrugged miserably and studied the gourmet food going cold on his mother's china. "He's so completely himself. Everything he says or does, he says and does with such total integrity. He's completely, purely Corbin. He almost seems—this is silly, I know. He seems like he lives in a different world. I don't just mean his own fantasy world. I mean, he seems like a creature from another place."

He thought Gareth might laugh, but Gareth nodded.

"There's something about him that just . . . it *calls* out to me. I've never felt that about anyone before. It's like a place inside him is screaming my name, and I just want to answer it with everything."

"Jesus."

Alex cringed and shook his head.

"No, sorry. I mean, damn, that's . . . that's something. You have to tell him, man."

"What if I ruin it? I'm so happy when I get to be around him. Everything feels fresh and new and fucking magical. What if I'm wrong and he never wants to see me again? The stakes feel high."

"Yeah, they should feel high, because you care a lot."

"I don't know if he's even interested in sex."

"You should tell him how you feel and you can ask him. Is it a deal breaker if he's not?"

Alex considered it. There were a lot of ways relationships could go. Infinite options for each element. "No. Not a deal breaker."

"Alex. If you tell him and he bolts, that will be awful. But . . . sorry to break it to you: you're an absolute horror to be around right now. You're kicking off pheromones like last call at the only bar in town, and you don't pay attention to anything but the kid when he's in the room."

"He's not a kid."

Gareth raised one eyebrow as if that had just made his point. "Talk to him. Soon. You owe him a chance to tell you how he feels."

And though Alex knew Gareth was playing on his sense of honor, he couldn't help but respond to it. It wasn't until he was lying in bed later, dreaming up how he might confess feelings to a wild thing, that Alex realized Gareth had never answered his question about what had happened on his camping trip.

THE WEATHER HAD TURNED the corner on winter overnight, and Alex's teeth chattered as he let himself into And Son early the next morning. Though it wasn't quite five yet, when he got into the kitchen, Corbin was already there and the smell of oil and fried dough hung in the air.

He said good morning, and Corbin just smiled at him, a sweet, preoccupied smile that made Alex forget anything he might've prepared to say.

The next day, Corbin was there before him again, and the day after, and each time, he looked at Alex with an uncharacteristic happiness, a hopefulness that took Alex's breath away.

A few days later, Corbin wasn't scheduled to come in until noon. As Alex stirred batters, whipped cream, and kneaded bread, he felt an unfamiliar sensation. Working on his own in kitchens had always filled him with an intense peace—a calm rivaled only by long walks in the woods before anyone was awake. It was one of the reasons he'd gravitated toward baking in the first place, rather than cooking. When your job began in the dark, it carried with it the stillness and joy of the rising sun, the waking city. For the first time, though, Alex felt lonely. He wished Corbin were there.

A little before noon, Corbin came into the kitchen with the wild smell of the wind and the trees on him. He moved like a sleepwalker and his eyes were hazy. He drifted closer and closer to Alex until there was no distance between them at all. Then he leaned in and kissed Alex on the cheek.

Electricity shot through Alex's body at the press of Corbin's lips, but was quieted by the fuzz of comfort at the feel of Corbin's eyelashes fluttering against his cheek. Alex stayed perfectly still, afraid he might scare Corbin away. But Corbin eased backward with a hand on Alex's shoulder and continued on his path, taking off his coat and dropping his bag in the corner, before tying on his apron as if nothing had happened.

"A POP-UP CHANUKAH DINNER!" Gareth said excitedly to Corbin as Alex mixed walnut bread.

"Pop up," Corbin echoed uncomprehendingly.

"It's when you set up a temporary restaurant for just a night or two," Alex explained.

Alex and Gareth had hatched the plan the night before, after Alex came home to find Gareth deboning a chicken to make chicken ballotine with pancetta, sage, and cornbread stuffing. Gareth clearly had some demons he was sublimating into his cooking, and Alex wanted to do something in And Son to thank everyone who'd welcomed him, and get to know the other local business owners outside the auspices of Mac's color-coded better business binders. So he would put Gareth's manic food energy to good use, and have a Chanukah dinner.

"Gareth can cook and I can do dessert. We can bring some of the old tables and chairs out of storage and set up in the café. We'll invite my mom and Lou, Lou's son, my employees, and some of the local business owners."

"Yeah, the ones we don't despise," Gareth muttered.

"Do you want me to help with dessert," Corbin asked.

"Sure, but really, Gareth was trying to tell you that we want you to come to the dinner."

Corbin froze. "I don't really do that."

"I know you don't. But would you want to come anyway?"

"Okay," Corbin said to the ground, and Gareth shot him a pointed look.

"Great, that's great. We're going to do it for the first night of Chanukah. It's early enough this year that it won't bump into Christmas, so people should be free."

Gareth left a few minutes later, and Corbin seemed out of sorts all day. He bumped into things and nearly spilled things, and he kept rubbing at his eyes, leaving streaks of flour and chocolate on his face.

Finally, worried he'd burn or cut himself, Alex caught Corbin's wrist. "What's wrong today?" He forced his voice to be gentle. Up close, he could see the dark circles under Corbin's eyes.

"I've just been working something out," Corbin murmured.

"Can you tell me what?"

Corbin trembled and his eyes slid shut for a moment.

"No. Not right now."

"Will you ever?" Alex found he wanted to know what Corbin was thinking about, what he was worried about or struggling with, more than he'd thought possible. He wanted to open Corbin up and pluck the thoughts from his brain. He wanted to help.

A tip of Corbin's head, a swallow. Then Corbin breathed, "I hope so."

OVER THE NEXT WEEK, as Gareth poured his fidgety energy into menu planning and recipe testing, Alex went up and down Main Street, inviting people to Chanukah dinner.

His mother was thrilled about the idea, and when he asked her to invite Lou, her eyes went soft and she squeezed his arm.

"I'm going to move in with him, Alex. Not right away, but soonish. We'll have to talk about what we're going to do with the house."

Alex's throat tightened like he'd swallowed too much of something very cold. Scraps of grief drifted up, sometimes, and he cleared his throat around them. His father had been a joyful man, and happiness had been what he'd wanted most for those he cared about. Alex had always known it. One of the reasons he'd felt ashamed it had taken him so long to tell his parents he was gay was that he knew his father would, in retrospect, see evidence that he'd been less than happy.

"I'm so glad for you, Mom," Alex said. "I'm glad you're happy. Just let me know what you want to do about the house. It's your call. Whenever you're ready." Her eyes welled up at the idea of leaving the house, but she nodded and hugged him tight.

The next day, Alex went to the Art Association to invite Lou's son to the Chanukah dinner. He'd meant to stop by and visit Orin before then, but with Gareth coming to town and Corbin eclipsing most everything else, he'd never found the time.

Downstairs in the gallery to the left, artists from across the state showcased their work. Paintings, silk scarves, felted tapestries, birdhouses of reclaimed wood, and jewelry made of every imaginable material. To the right was an empty studio space, the scattered drop cloths and can lights suggesting a show was in the middle of being put up.

The steep, wooden staircase between the two spaces was what Alex remembered from a long time ago. When he'd climbed it before, it had been the peeling slate blue of a beach house porch. Now it was painted a glossy teal.

Upstairs, a horseshoe-shaped attic space was organized into sections: easels and paints, pottery wheels and kiln, mixed materials and tools. There was a group of five or six kids who looked about ten years old in the painting section, for what must have been an after-school class, and a young woman with long brown hair was walking among the easels, helping them.

There were two men in worn clothing with packs at their feet, sitting on a carpet-covered ledge by the arched window that had a view onto Liberty Street. One seemed almost asleep sitting up and the other was turning a hand-rolled cigarette over and over in his fingers, knee bouncing.

Alex found Orin in the cluttered office in the back corner of the space. Papers were on every available surface, and he looked up from wrestling with a printer cable when Alex knocked.

Alex sketched a wave. "I hope it's okay I stopped by."

"Yeah, sure." Orin clambered to his feet and shook Alex's hand. He looked hassled and tired, and there was an awkward beat where they stood there staring at each other.

"So, I think my mom and your dad are going to shack up," Alex said.

Orin raised an eyebrow at *shack up* but nodded. He clearly

wasn't going to say anything else on the matter, so Alex cut to the chase and extended the invitation to Chanukah dinner.

"My friend Gareth will be cooking and I'll be doing dessert. Corbin will help."

Alex felt his cheeks heat at the realization that there had been no need to offer that detail about Corbin. He'd said Corbin's name just to hear it, just to feel connected to him.

"Corbin Wale?" Alex nodded. "I'm glad."

"Glad?"

Orin crossed his arms and leaned his hip against the cluttered desk, considering Alex. Finally, he said, "Two years ago or so, I was walking to the Potters Guild sale on the weekend. There was a little store across the street, then. It's closed now, but it used to sell jam and honey and little jars of other expensive crap."

Alex smiled.

"I saw this kid—I thought he was real young, anyway— standing just inside the door that was propped open. The lady who owned the shop was screaming at him, and there was broken glass and globs of jam all around his feet. And the kid—Corbin— was staring into space like he didn't even hear her."

Alex's stomach lurched at the thought of someone yelling at Corbin, of that aggression ruffling his delicate senses.

"I stopped because I swear I thought that lady might do him harm with the broom or something, but Corbin turned in the doorway and walked out, like he'd heard his mama calling him home for dinner. And she just kept hollering at him as he walked away, calling him useless and crazy."

Alex gritted his teeth. The word *crazy* was starting to make him flinch.

"At the end of the block, he stopped and stood there like he wasn't sure which way to go. I went over to him and asked if he was okay, if he needed help." Orin shrugged. "I used to work with folks who had some mental health stuff going on, and I thought maybe . . . Anyway, he gazed at me like he couldn't figure out what I was saying. Then he snapped back into focus so quickly. He seemed embarrassed and he said, 'I'm probably fired, right.'" Orin chuckled. "I laughed and said, 'Yeah, I think you're done,' and he cracked a grin and said, 'Good. Her jam tasted like Fruit Loops.'"

Alex was flooded with fondness for this years ago version of Corbin he'd never known.

"I walked with him a ways and we exchanged names and I told him I was going to the Potters Guild sale and he said . . ." Orin looked down self-consciously. "He pointed at my hands and said, 'You seem like a potter. Your hands change whatever they touch.' And then he walked away."

Orin was staring at his own hands, as if seeing whatever Corbin saw. They were large and graceful, with the suggestion of an easy strength.

"People aren't kind to him," Alex said, but found he could hardly get the words out around a lump in his throat. It was such a simple truth and it hit Alex with a wallop. "They haven't ever been kind to him."

"No," Orin agreed. "It leaves a mark, all that unkindness. I think that's part of what I saw in him."

Alex thought perhaps Orin himself had known a great deal of unkindness, and knew equally well that he wouldn't wish to have it mentioned.

"You worked with people who . . ." Alex trailed off. He wasn't sure what question he was trying to form. "Corbin's not . . . He sees the world differently but—"

Orin held out a quelling hand. "I know. It's good he has people to be kind to him now. I'm glad of it." He paused, jaw working for a moment. "If someone is living their life the way they wish, and the way they wish doesn't harm anyone, there's nothing to say. It's easier to see if someone *is* causing harm, or can't function. The tricky situations are when people themselves doesn't know that their lives could be different. When they don't have the information to make the choice. I don't know Corbin. It seems like maybe you do, a little. He's the only one who can answer that question. I'm glad you know to ask it, rather than to tell him the answers."

The moment was sown between them, the seed of accord that could blossom into friendship.

"Thank you," Alex said. "For your thoughts, and for helping Corbin back then. I . . ." He shook his head, amazed that he could say to a near-stranger what Gareth had practically had to drag out of him. "I care for Corbin a lot. I don't want to do anything to hurt him, and I don't want to take advantage because I don't understand. This helped."

Orin clasped his hand, this time bringing him in for a quick press of shoulders and a thump on the back. "I'm glad. I'm glad about your mother, too. My dad, he's . . . real easy to like. Sometimes it makes people think that's all he is. But your mom, she sees him clearly, even the parts that aren't so easy."

They smiled at each other, and Alex recognized an ally.

Chapter Thirteen

CORBIN SEEMED to be in a good mood. "Good mood" wasn't something Alex had ever thought to ascribe to him, since the good/bad spectrum wasn't one that Corbin's moods seemed to fall on. But this morning, he seemed unusually light, almost buoyant.

When he looked up at Alex and smiled easily, it took Alex's breath away.

"I found someone for you," Corbin said. "Maybe."

"Some*one*?"

Corbin nodded. "I can show you after, if you want."

"Yeah, okay."

At another moment, with another person, Alex would have said *Who is it?* And *Just tell me what it is now.* Alex liked to be able to plan ahead. But he found that with Corbin, he loved the way ordinary things unfolded like tiny mysteries. As much as he recognized his desire to know everything about Corbin, he also enjoyed not knowing until Corbin decided it was time to tell him. He enjoyed that something had made Corbin smile, and Corbin would hold it close to him as they baked, until later.

After work, Alex drove them to Corbin's house. Corbin's mouth stayed tipped up in the corners, like he was just waiting for something to push it into a full smile.

Snow blanketed Corbin's yard and garden, and he tramped through it toward the back of the house. As soon as Corbin was there, Wolf trotted out of the trees.

"Where is she," Corbin asked Wolf. Wolf turned his head toward the trees and barked twice. A few moments later came the sound of cracking twigs and rustling leaves, and a dog shot out of the trees and cannoned toward them. It was medium-sized, with shaggy black-and-white fur, and a goofy, hopeful face. When it reached Corbin, it skidded to a halt and vibrated with excitement.

Corbin held up a hand, and the dog started bouncing in circles, spinning around and around before crashing to the ground dizzily.

Alex laughed and Corbin smiled. He pointed at the dog and said, "I thought she might be right for you."

Warmth flooded Alex's chest. Corbin had found him a dog. Corbin had remembered that he might want one, had met one, and thought of Alex.

"How did you know she'd be right?" he asked.

"I just knew," Corbin said, and it was clear he remembered their conversation in Alex's kitchen as well as Alex did. "I accidentally named her," Corbin said, scuffing at the ground. He said it like a name was unchangeable, and Alex realized that to him, it was.

"That's okay. What's her name, then?"

"Dreidel," Corbin said, and held out his hand to the dog. Again, she jumped up and spun in circles like a top before collapsing. This time she looked up at Alex and crooked a paw. He reached out slowly and squeezed the snow-cold paw, then ran his palm over her fur. She shivered with pleasure and splayed out on her back.

"She's perfect," Alex said. "It's the perfect name."

Corbin bounced slightly on his toes, and his bright smile was so singularly sweet that Alex stood and hugged him. "Thank you," he said, and Corbin, who'd stiffened at first, softened, letting himself be held. Then his arms came up around Alex's shoulders, tentative at first, then hanging on tight.

By mutual unspoken agreement, they went inside. Wolf settled near the kitchen door, and Corbin held the door open for Dreidel. She bolted inside, tracking dirtied snow across the hardwood floor, and spun around in excited circles a few times. Corbin spoke to her softly and wiped off her paws with a towel hanging inside the door. Then he grabbed a bowl from the kitchen and filled it with Stick's food, which Dreidel inhaled.

In the living room, Corbin kindled a fire and gestured for Alex to sit. After a few minutes, Dreidel galloped into the living room. She spun around again, then collapsed in front of the fire, and fell almost instantly asleep.

Corbin brought them hot tea and settled onto the other side of the couch from Alex. He tucked his knees up and cradled the warm cup, letting the steam warm his face.

"Everything for the Chanukah dinner is coming together," Alex said. "I've invited people, and Gareth's gone through four different menu concepts, but whatever he lands on will be delicious."

Corbin nodded, relaxing into the couch like he was content to listen to Alex run through all the details. Like he'd be content to listen to whatever Alex had to say.

"I invited Orin." Corbin cocked his head and wrinkled his brow. "He runs the Art Association. The potter?"

"Oh. Yes, I've met him."

"Yeah, he told me." Alex spoke casually, choosing his words carefully. "He said you weren't very impressed with a certain shopkeeper's jam."

Corbin nodded immediately. "That jam was horrible. My aunts used to make jam. I know how jam should taste. That tasted terrible."

Alex smiled at his strong opinion on the matter. "What's your favorite kind of jam?" He realized that he knew hardly anything about the small, particular details of Corbin's life.

"Favorite. I don't really have a favorite. There are infinite combinations."

"That's true. You might not even have tasted your favorite yet."

"Yes, exactly," Corbin said, and his face fell into an expression that Alex had come to think of as satisfaction that Alex had understood.

"If you had all the ingredients in the world in your kitchen and you were going to go in there right now and make jam, do you know what kind you would make?"

"Mmm." Corbin closed his eyes like he was picturing every ingredient in the world. "Peach and ginger."

"That sounds good. Orin said that woman was saying some pretty rude things to you when you left," Alex said softly.

Corbin's eyes were narrowed, and his gaze leveled Alex. His voice was sharper than Alex had ever heard it. "Yes. People think I'm crazy. Didn't you know." The word *crazy* snapped around them. Alex didn't like it, but Corbin was clearly repeating what people had said to him.

"Others too?" Alex asked gently.

Corbin put his tea on the ground and leaned his head back over the arm of the couch to stare at the ceiling. "Yes."

He was quiet for long enough that Alex thought he would say more. Then he said, "The teachers at school. They thought something was wrong with me. Because I didn't always pay attention. But I was paying attention. To other things. I was drawing or reading. There were all these rules and everyone knew them, but they didn't make any sense to me."

Alex wasn't surprised to hear that, given that Corbin had grown up outside the context of school. He'd never have learned what was expected of students, or that rules were just edicts kids were meant to follow and often had no discernible logic.

"They would say to read something or fill words in blanks, but . . . why. We all stood up and sat down and raised our hands and walked to the next place, but none of it meant anything."

Corbin looked so confused.

"Aunt Hilda said that we just had to play along. People were stupid and they needed rules to feel like their lives made sense, so I should just go through the motions until I could get out of there and then I could do whatever I wanted."

The sweater Corbin was wearing was the same one he'd worn

to Alex's house, and Corbin picked at the loose fibers in the cuff as he spoke.

"I tried to go along with it. But they wouldn't leave me alone. The other students wouldn't leave me alone. And the teachers kept asking me things they didn't ask anyone else. Mr. Bashir sent me to the guidance counselor and she . . . she scared me."

Corbin turned haunted eyes toward Alex.

"She said I was crazy."

"She *said* that to you?"

"Not that word. But that's what she meant. It's what they always meant. They thought I didn't know, but I knew. She called my aunts and told them I needed tests. That something was wrong with me. They were furious. They said she couldn't make me. But then . . . I got scared that if I didn't, then someone might take me away from home."

His voice was small, and he wrapped his arms around his legs, hugging himself.

"I told the lady I'd take her test. It was . . . The thing was that . . . those questions. It—they scared me."

"What were the questions?"

Corbin shook his head. "Just questions. They didn't mean the same thing to me that they'd meant to her. But I knew that if I told the truth she would think she was right. That there was something wrong with me."

Alex's heart started beating faster. "Do *you* think there's something wrong with you?"

Corbin bit at his fingernails.

"It's not wrong with *me*," he said finally. "It's just . . . wrong."

"I'm not sure what that means, Corbin."

"I can't tell you because you'll think I'm crazy too," Corbin said. He got up off the couch and sat down in front of the fire, both hands on Dreidel, working the tangles out of her fur.

Alex wasn't sure what to think about that. Corbin felt intensely *right* to him. There was clearly something he felt he couldn't share, but everything in Alex told him it wasn't anything bad or wrong. He thought about what Orin had said. That the tricky part was when someone didn't know that they could be different than they were. But Corbin *did* seem to know that there were other ways to live—that most people lived differently, in fact.

"Maybe you'll tell me some other time," Alex said slowly. "I'd like to hear anything you might want to tell me."

Corbin looked at him for a long time, the firelight flickering in his hair like a reflection in obsidian. "You would," he said finally, and Alex couldn't tell if it was a statement or a question.

"I would," he said, just to be safe.

"Maybe soon," Corbin murmured. "If I figure it out."

SOFT HANDS RAN up and down Alex's thighs, spreading his legs, and hair whispered against his erection. Alex groaned and looked down to see Corbin's face between his legs, pink tongue in a wicked point coming out to lick the tip of Alex's cock. Alex reached out a trembling hand to push back Corbin's hair, but the second he touched him, the bed disappeared and they were floating. Corbin's wings, the feathers as ink-black as his hair, spread around him, and Alex felt the air quiver with energy.

The tips of Corbin's feathers caressed Alex's ribs and flanks, leaving trails of fire in their wake. Alex's eyes were glued to Corbin's face. His eyes were dark with lust, his cheeks flushed, and his mouth a slick fantasy. Corbin's eyelashes fluttered, and he swallowed Alex's cock to the root. The pleasure was oceanic, and he came in Corbin's mouth in seconds, every muscle tensed as pulse after pulse of pleasure spewed from him like lava.

Alex woke with a gasp to sweat-soaked sheets and sticky

underwear, his chest heaving with release and the image of Corbin taking him into his body making him groan all over again.

"Jesus."

He threw his underwear in the laundry and stood naked by the window, gazing out into the dark. Black boughs of fir trees bobbed in the wind, and a light snow was falling, just visible in the circle of a streetlight.

The night before, at Corbin's house, after the disturbing talk about the high school guidance counselor, they'd moved on to speak of other things. They'd agreed that Dreidel would stay at Corbin's for the moment, until Alex knew what his mother wanted to do with the house. They talked about what they should serve for dessert at the Chanukah dinner.

The traditional desserts, fried in oil, were a bit heavy for the end of a meal, and they would be things Alex was selling at And Son for the whole holiday season. They debated the merits of something light and refreshing—fruit and cream and sorbets. But though they would be a good counterbalance to the rich dinner menu, they didn't really have the spirit of Chanukah celebration that Alex was after. Besides, though Gareth's menu would be rich, it—like everything he cooked—would be balanced, so it wouldn't feel heavy.

It was Corbin who'd had the idea Alex liked best. It was a deconstructed sufganiyot and Corbin had thought of it because of their talk about jam. They would layer the cinnamon and sugar doughnuts with vanilla cream and fresh jam. Alex could already see how he'd plate it, the jam drizzled over the cream so the doughnuts would stay crisp.

He shook his head. Everything in it led back to Corbin. Even baking was now all wrapped up with Corbin.

Gareth was right. Alex had to tell him. If not for his own sake, then because he was starting to feel uncomfortable being around Corbin in person, when at night, the private Corbin of his dreams caressed and sucked him to ecstasy, and made him come in his sleep like he was seventeen again.

He'd just wait until the next week, see the Chanukah dinner through, and then he'd talk to Corbin. His stomach clenched at how easily the other man could slip from his life if he didn't feel the same. How easily Alex could be left.

The emptiness he felt at the thought of losing Corbin—of not seeing his beautiful smile, or the way he tugged at his hair when it got in his face, of how he shifted between dreamy distraction and a presence so sharp it drew every ounce of Alex's attention, of his scent like the wildness of the trees and the wind—was stronger than anything he'd ever felt.

GARETH WAS CHATTERING EXCITEDLY about the menu as they drove to the bakery the morning before the Chanukah dinner. Everything was planned, and he'd do the shopping today. They were both delighted with the pie he'd dreamt up. It would have a crust of shredded, fried potato filled with apples and drizzled with a sour cream—his play on latkes with applesauce and sour cream, and an elegant solution to the problem of how to fry a hundred latkes while people waited to be served.

Gareth was describing how he'd absorb the oil of the potato when they let themselves into And Son and found the kitchen light on.

Gareth shot Alex a look. When Alex had told him how often he'd found Corbin in the kitchen before him, Gareth had said with certainty that it was yet another indication that he liked Alex and wanted to be near him. Alex thought there was something more to it, but didn't know what.

Alex pushed open the door quietly, and the sight before him stole his breath. Corbin was asleep on the butcher-block prep table in the corner, hands curled under his chin, head pillowed on his jacket. In sleep, he looked as he did in Alex's dreams. Beautiful, angelic, at peace.

Gareth hung back and Alex went over to him. "Corbin," he said softly, putting a hand on the man's shoulder in case he startled and fell off the table.

Corbin blinked awake and Alex's heart sped knowing that now he could picture what it would look like to wake up next to him. Corbin's mouth formed a silent *Alex*, and he sat, knuckling sleep from his eyes.

"I fell asleep," he muttered.

"Did you come here last night?"

Corbin shook his head. "Early this morning." Then a smile broke across his face. "I made something."

He scrambled off the counter and lifted a kitchen towel from a plate. They were sufganiyot, perfectly formed, fried, and filled.

"Wow, they're beautiful. Were you practicing?"

Corbin cocked his head. "No. They're for you." His voice was grave.

"Thank you," Alex said seriously, though it was a little earlier than he usually wanted to eat. But Corbin was staring at him, eyes wide and hair mussed, with the impression of his jacket creasing his cheek, and Alex didn't think he had it in him to deny him anything. So he took the doughnut that Corbin held out to him like a communion.

He took a bite and the flavors burst across his sleepy palate. The crunch of cinnamon and sugar, the crisp of fried dough as his teeth sank in, and the bite of jam inside—blueberry, perfect with the cinnamon.

"It's perfect," Alex said, and Corbin's smile turned everything to joy. He bounced on his toes, waiting as Alex finished the doughnut.

"Do I get one?" Gareth asked. "Or are they special magic doughnuts for Alex's consumption only?" He winked at Corbin, but Corbin's face fell and he looked gutted.

He put the towel back over the doughnuts and shook his head. "I'm sorry. But you can't have one." His hands shook.

Alex glared at Gareth, who rolled his eyes. "It's fine, Corbin. It's fine if they're special magic doughnuts only for Alex."

Corbin flinched again, eyes darting around.

"Hey," Alex said, squeezing Corbin's shoulder. "Thank you. They're delicious. I love the choice of blueberry jam. It works perfectly with the cinnamon and it's less expected."

Corbin nodded.

"I'm gonna go shopping," Gareth said, and spun on his heel.

As soon as he was gone, Corbin seemed to relax. He looked at the doughnuts and at Alex. "It's just . . . no one else can have them, okay? It's important."

"Okay." Alex let the word linger between them, hoping Corbin would explain, but knowing he might not. If Corbin said something was important to him, that was all Alex needed.

"I'm . . . I'm trying to make things so that I can tell you. So I can tell you all the things you keep asking."

"Is it working?"

The expression on Corbin's face was naked longing.

"I think maybe so," he whispered in awe.

Chapter Fourteen

AS HE FLIPPED the sign on the front door from Open to Closed, and taped up the card that said *Private Event*, Alex was suspended perfectly between a childlike joy of Chanukah cheer and a professional baker's desire for perfection. He liked the position just fine.

Gareth was putting the finishing touches on all the food and giving exacting instructions to the waiters they'd hired for the evening about how and when each course was to be served.

Alex was quite used to Gareth's high standards and knew that he'd tip generously, but his manner had Corbin as skittish as the first day Alex had met him.

"It's okay," Alex reassured him. "He'll calm down as soon as people taste the first dish and ooh and ah over it."

But Corbin didn't seem calmed. In fact, Corbin had been skittish all day. His head popped up at every noise, and Alex had felt his eyes on him from across the room. It was almost like Corbin was waiting for something.

Mira and Sean had spent every minute they weren't serving customers during the day decorating the shop. Alex had wanted it to look festive but not garish, and he thought they'd hit the mark perfectly. Blue and silver garland draped the counter, and on the tables were centerpieces of glass bells that held glittery blue and silver stars. At the door, a blue-draped table was laid with dreidels and bags of chocolate gelt. They'd covered the counter in blue velvet and turned it into a bar, with one of the servers bartending behind it.

All in all, it looked cozy and festive, and Alex couldn't have been happier.

True to form, his mother and Lou were the first to arrive, arm in arm.

"I can't believe it's the same place," she exclaimed for what had to be the dozenth time since he'd opened, and Lou shook his hand and echoed the sentiment.

"Corbin!" his mom said excitedly, and Alex turned to see Corbin, who had been creeping out of the kitchen, suddenly freeze under her attention. But when she approached him, smiled warmly, and held out her arms for a hug, Corbin walked into them without hesitation, and let himself be held.

Something fluttered in Alex's throat. Envy. That Corbin could so easily touch someone who wasn't him.

More guests arrived and Alex shook the envy off, introducing everyone who wasn't already acquainted and passing around drinks.

When Orin arrived, Alex was legitimately happy to see him. "You remember Corbin?" he said, and Orin shook Corbin's hand solemnly and smiled.

"I'm glad to see you again," he said.

Alex tugged Gareth over, too. "This is Orin Wright, Lou's son. He runs the Art Association I told you about. Orin, this is my best friend, Gareth Kelly. He's a chef. He prepared the food for tonight."

Orin's eyes were locked on Gareth, and he held out a hand as if in slow motion. Gareth's trembled slightly as he took it. "Pleasure to meet you," Orin said, voice low and rough, as Gareth said, "Hey."

Alex caught Corbin's gaze over their clasped hands, and Corbin's eyebrows went up, his eyes widening. Alex winked and inclined his head, and he took Corbin to the bar and got him a drink, putting himself between Corbin and the growing crowd.

"You don't need to protect me," Corbin said, gesturing to the people milling around. "They think I'm a freak, but I'm used to it. This has been my whole life." He scuffed his toe, eyes glued to the ground.

"What if I do need to?" Alex asked, something about the festivities making him bolder with Corbin than he ever had been. He had never felt like it was his right to exert any control over his partners. He had known his whole life that people tended to do what he said.

You sounded like you knew what you were talking about, his college boyfriend said when he offered a wild theory, *so I believed you.*

You said it like you were sure, his friend insisted, lost in North Carolina after Alex had said he thought that *maybe, possibly*, that highway would take them to Durham.

Gareth hadn't been the first to notice it, just the first to point out the pattern to Alex. Alex had already known that if he swept in and simply took care of things, people tended to let him. Even if they didn't actually want to.

But though he usually kept the impulse in check, he still burned sometimes with the desire to take control of things, set them to rights. It felt like if he could just reach his hands in to the heart of the problem and put the pieces back together—if his friends and lovers would just relax and let themselves float while he tinkered—he could fix it all.

Ego much? Gareth had said when Alex had once told him this. Alex knew it was true. And yet, he still felt it. He saw Corbin suffering from the sidelong looks and whispers, and he wanted to step between him and those things, take the blow. And he wanted Corbin to want him to. Needed him to.

"Why would you need to," Corbin asked, but his pupils dilated, and Alex thought he saw him swallow hard.

"I feel very protective of you, Corbin. It's just how I am. Does it bother you?"

Corbin blinked wide eyes and peered at Alex, a flush creeping up from the neck of his sweater.

"No."

An answering heat kindled in Alex, low in the pit of his stomach.

Corbin opened his mouth like he was about to speak, when

Gareth clapped Alex on the shoulder and said, "It's time." Gareth could feel the energy of a crowd and know when food or drink or neither were needed.

"Okay," Alex said, and signaled the server standing by the kitchen. To Corbin he said, "You'll sit with us, right?" He held out a hand, wanting so badly for Corbin to take it easily, the way he'd shaken Orin's hand or hugged his mother. Corbin stared at it, narrowed eyes flicking up to Alex's face like he was reading something only he could see. Then, slowly, he slid his hand into Alex's, blinking quickly at the contact.

Alex felt the disarrangement inside his chest ease.

At his table sat Corbin, his mother, Lou, Gareth, and Orin. His mother and Lou were smiley and bright-eyed, turning in their chairs to talk to everyone, even the servers.

Gareth and Orin spoke intermittently, their eyes locked, but their gazes roamed over each other when the other wasn't looking.

Corbin sat beside him, occasionally talking to Orin, answering the questions his mother asked, but mostly leaning, as the dinner progressed, closer to Alex, inch by inch, as if he didn't realize he was doing it.

Alex looked around at what he'd built and felt a surge of pride. He couldn't believe how utterly different his life was than it had been mere months before. The impact of the change had perhaps not quite caught up with him until this moment, when he sat at the middle of a group he was now a part of.

The food was wonderful, and though Gareth's nostrils occasionally flared when the plating was not precisely what he'd asked for, people were clearly enjoying it. The latke-crust apple pie with sour cream was the hit of the night, and Gareth endured more praise for his cleverness than he was used to. Ann Arbor consumers were not New York City diners, and Alex could read his pleasure, and then his annoyance, on his face.

After the pie, there were delicate cheese blintzes with chive and horseradish mustard, and a salad of spicy arugula, roasted golden beets, and slivered fig. The main course was braised brisket kreplach dotted with a minted pea puree and watercress, the dumplings firm and savory, the peas and cress light.

Gareth's eyes roamed the room to make sure people were enjoying it, and Alex forced himself not to grin when Gareth corrected Orin about what an ingredient was and then went on to explain every component of the dish in detail.

And through it all, he felt Corbin next to him, a welcome presence. He felt Corbin's curious eyes on him even as they ate.

When the plates were cleared away and more drinks had been passed around, Gareth signaled for dessert service.

"Corbin came up with the idea for dessert," Alex said to his mom, loudly enough that everyone could likely hear, and Corbin dropped his chin to his chest so his hair hid his face.

When the plates of sufganiyot, blueberry jam, and vanilla cream came out, Alex couldn't help but think of the container in his room at home that held the rest of the doughnuts that Corbin had made for him the morning before.

He'd eaten another in the afternoon, and yet another when he woke up this morning, and was, frankly, sick of doughnuts. But Corbin had made them especially for him, and it had clearly meant something to Corbin to see him eat one. Alone in his bedroom, as if he were hiding a secret in his own home, Alex had closed his eyes as he'd eaten another, chewing slowly and picturing Corbin's hands all over them. Corbin's hands kneading the dough and stamping them out. Corbin's hands smothering them in cinnamon sugar. Corbin's hands running over blueberries and choosing the juiciest ones for jam. Corbin covering them with a towel to keep them just for him.

He'd allowed himself to imagine they were something more than dessert. That Corbin had offered Alex a proxy for himself. Then he'd imagined those same hands all over *him* and felt a tug low in his belly. Along with it had come a yearning—the kind of desire that wells up in search of answering desire. He wanted to consume Corbin's sweetness just as he'd consumed each bite.

By the time dessert plates were scraped clean and the dregs of drinks quaffed, Alex was ready for everyone to leave. The air of celebration kept people around for another hour, playing dreidel and talking about the holidays. Alex was glad Chanukah had fallen early this year so that he could have this without it being swallowed up by Christmas, as it was the years they coincided.

His mother caught his elbow. "This was wonderful, Aly" She hadn't called him that in years, and Alex leaned down to see tears in her eyes. "Your dad would've loved it. He would've loved seeing you here—this place—everything you've done."

He hugged her, smelling the familiar scent of her shampoo and the perfume she'd worn since he was a child.

"I can't believe I'm here. I wish he could see it too."

She pulled him down to kiss his forehead, then left, Lou on her arm.

Soon, everyone was gone, and the servers were clearing the room, evidence of the festivities swept away as if they'd never occurred.

Gareth slid an arm around his waist. "Was it Chanukah-y enough for you? Did it feel the way you wanted?"

It was teasing, but there was a tenderness to Gareth's voice that touched him.

"It was wonderful. The food was perfect. Thank you." He squeezed Gareth's shoulder. "I don't know if I would ever have opened this place if it hadn't been for you encouraging me that day."

"You would have," Gareth said with certainty. And he was probably right. "Um, listen, I'm gonna take off, okay? I'll catch up with you soon."

"Are you not going back to the house?" Alex asked, but then he followed Gareth's eye line to where Orin stood just outside the bakery, hands shoved in his pockets and shoulders raised against the cold. "Ah. Gotcha. I like him."

"Whatever, I don't need your approval," Gareth muttered. Then, "Yeah?"

"Yeah. I mean, I like him as person. I don't know how he'll be for you. Just . . . be careful, okay?"

Gareth's sigh contained everything unspoken. "I'll try. I'm not very good at it. Being careful."

"Well, be as careful as you can be, and I'll fuck him up if he hurts you, how's that?"

"That's perfect," Gareth said, and they both knew Alex wouldn't hurt Orin. It was just how he expressed his care.

Alex found Corbin pressed to the corner of the kitchen, clearly trying to stay far out of the servers' way as they cleaned up. Alex's head was throbbing and he was exhausted. All he wanted was quiet. And Corbin.

"Hey, you all did a great job," he called to the servers. "I'll finish cleaning up tomorrow. You can take off, if Gareth paid you?" They nodded and scattered before he could change his mind.

Then Alex and Corbin were alone, the wreckage of the kitchen disappearing around them as their eyes locked. Alex went to Corbin as if he couldn't possibly do anything else, and Corbin breathed deeply, like he was smelling him.

Alex was tired and a little tipsy, and Corbin was the most beautiful, most precious thing he'd ever seen. He put one hand on Corbin's shoulder and felt muscle and bone beneath his skin. He put the other at Corbin's neck, needing to feel the texture of his skin, the throb of his pulse.

Corbin's eyes fluttered shut and his breathing was shallow, but he didn't pull away.

"Happy Chanukah," Alex said. At Corbin's small, pleased smile, Alex opened his mouth and let the words escape, whatever they might be. He was done holding back, done censoring. "You're a miracle to me, Corbin." Alex's heart pounded when he heard what he'd said, but he didn't take the words back. He'd meant them completely.

Corbin's eyes flew open, searching Alex's face.

"I know it's a little corny," Alex went on, "but I've always loved the holidays because there's something magical about them to me." Corbin's eyes flared, but he still didn't speak. "It's a time when the whole world seems different. People are kinder to each other, happier. They do things they might not ordinarily do, connect with people they might never speak to otherwise. And what is magic if not the possibility for things to happen that would otherwise be impossible?"

Corbin gaped, and his hands came up to fist the fabric of Alex's shirt. The color in his cheeks was high, his eyes brighter than Alex had ever seen them.

"Corbin," Alex murmured. And he imagined that Corbin had been right when he said that a name gives power over the named. He imagined that he could speak Corbin's name over and over until the man was his. "Corbin," he said again, leaning closer. Corbin's breath caught.

Alex cupped Corbin's face in his hands, searching those dark eyes for a sign that this was welcome, that he was wanted. He saw such desire there, such need, that it rocked him to his core.

"You're so beautiful," he said, running his fingers down Corbin's throat. "Corbin, god."

He could feel the flutter of Corbin's racing pulse, and Corbin's hands tightened on his shirt as if he thought Alex might pull away. The closer Alex leaned, the tighter Corbin held him, until they were pressed together, Corbin's fists the only thing between them. Alex could smell woodsmoke in Corbin's hair.

Then Corbin flattened his palms to Alex's chest and it felt like the last thing between them dissolved. Alex cradled the back of Corbin's head and the side of his neck and leaned closer, closer, until their lips brushed, and the sensation of it blasted through him like lightning. Corbin made a small, desperate sound in the back of his throat and Alex surged forward, kissing him with everything he had.

Their mouths crushed together. The kiss was frantic and clumsy and everything that Alex had ever wanted. Beneath the hint of blueberries, Alex could taste the wild, winter flavor of Corbin himself, and he'd never tasted anything so intoxicating.

Corbin's hands scrabbled at his back, pulling him closer, and he pressed his hips to Corbin's, feeling the hardness that answered his own. He groaned into Corbin's mouth and heard Corbin's broken whimper.

Then the whimper turned from arousal to something else, and Corbin shoved him away. Alex's eyes shot open to see Corbin, chest heaving, one hand clamped over his mouth and the other gripping the countertop he'd been pressed against. His eyes were panicked and his throat worked convulsively.

"Corbin?"

Corbin squeezed his eyes shut and shook his head over and over.

When Alex tried to touch him again, Corbin curled into himself. "You can't," he sobbed. Then, "Alex, you can't."

Panic gripped Alex as he stared at the empty space and his own outstretched hands. He didn't know what he'd done, but it had ripped Corbin from him, turning intimacy to distance and pleasure to fear. He'd reached for something gossamer, and he'd shredded it with rough hands. The most beautiful kiss he'd ever shared had turned to dust in his mouth.

"Why? What's wrong? Tell me, please."

"You—you—you can't understand, but . . ." He shook his head again. "I ruin everything I touch. Everyone I— I can't ruin you. I can't . . . I can't hurt you."

The words tore through Alex like a bullet. "Oh, baby, no." He moved toward Corbin again, but stopped himself at the fear he saw there.

"No, I will, I— I tried to fix it, but . . . I thought maybe I could make things okay, but what if— I can't risk it."

Before Alex could regroup, Corbin flew out the door.

Part Four 🌿 Fire

Corbin

Chapter Fifteen

CORBIN WONDERED if a heart could break and still beat away, trapped in the cage of ribs, no matter its extremity.

He walked through the wintry streets, letting himself be turned and twisted like a dry leaf in the breeze, his path toward home labyrinthine and untraceable.

For the last week, he'd taken his cue from the Chanukah story Alex had told him. It was a sign that the oil was what he needed to dispel the curse. The challah had been a good start, but the doughnuts would clinch it. He'd sent the curse into the dough, then singed batch after batch in boiling oil, waiting for the miracle. Waiting for a sign that this was right.

Finally, he'd *felt* something. Felt some lingering vestige of wrongness leave him, and he'd thought it was gone. Then, he'd made the last batch. Infused the dough with hope and joy, and fried them perfectly for Alex. *You should cook with love when you're cooking for someone you love.* Just for Alex.

And as he'd watched Alex take a bite, take part of Corbin's hope and joy into himself, he'd felt the universe snap into place like a rubber band.

All day today, he'd watched Alex for signs that it had worked. When Alex had touched him, he'd watched for signs that there had been no poison left to leach into the other man. No threat.

Alex had glowed as beautifully as he always did. There was no sickly tinge of black in the air around him, no hint of taint or hurt. There had been a bright red, just next to his skin. *Desire.* And when they'd kissed . . .

Corbin's whole body shuddered at the memory. That kiss . . . that kiss had remade him. Dragged him to the blackest sky and the brightest stars and exploded him into something he had never known. Alex's mouth and Alex's hands and Alex's body, yes, but mostly *Alex*. Alex wanting him, Alex needing him, Alex *with* him.

It was what he had always yearned for, and what he'd thought he could never have. That he'd had it, for just a few minutes, and then lost it, tore a sob from his throat that the wind snatched away.

Because Corbin couldn't be *sure* his miracle had worked. After all, what was he, with his makeshiftery, his ersatz spell craft, in the face of the curse that had dogged the Wales for generations? And if he hadn't broken the curse, and he let himself be with Alex, then Alex was doomed. But there was only one way to know for sure, and if he was wrong, it would be too late by then.

So he'd left.

He'd torn himself away, leaving the barest, neediest, most grasping parts of himself in Alex's outstretched hand.

Now everything was darkness and cold and wind, the only warmth the promise of home, which was dark and cold and empty.

"Finnian," he whispered, voice ragged. But Finnian didn't come because he wasn't the one Corbin really wanted. "Carbon?" No.

He didn't want any of them. He didn't want pieces or shades or lines on the page. He wanted flesh and blood and bone and sweat. Heart and cock and mouth. He wanted Alex. He would always want Alex.

The woods were dark in the new moon, spindly shadows looming. Night birds cawed, their calls spread thin and shriekish by the wind. There was no peace here tonight, no comfort from the plants and trees, their roots singing to each other, deep beneath the ground, a world of understanding with no words. His ears prickled and his feet felt numb. He considered, for a moment, never returning home.

No one would know. No one would miss him. If he cut to the bottom of things, the house was just a house, the garden just a garden, none of it holding him here the way it had held the aunts, cradled them. They had found their peace here, their moments of happiness, such as they were. It had been their succor against the world. Their sanctuary.

He had imagined it might be the same for him.

But there was no sanctuary anymore. He carried the storm inside him.

When the trees cleared on his back garden, he found Alex standing near the kitchen door, head hanging down, Wolf alert by his side.

He froze at the tree line, caught between longing and fear. Part of him wanted to step backward into the woods and lose himself in the darkness. But as Wolf sensed him, Alex's head jerked up, and in his face was suffering Corbin couldn't abide.

He walked slowly toward them, and Wolf relaxed. "Corbin," Alex said. Alex wouldn't stop saying his name, and every time he said it, the cords that bound them together tightened.

"We have to talk," Alex said. "Let me in? Please."

Requests and commands and desires and magic words.

"Okay," Corbin said, finally. "But . . . but you can't touch me. Not yet." *It's not safe; I won't risk you; please don't let me hurt you.*

Alex flinched and hung his head, but then he nodded, giving Corbin a wide berth as they went inside. Corbin made a fire, stacking the wood deliberately so he wouldn't have to speak. He was assessing the risk.

Finally, "Corbin," Alex said. He gave the fire one last poke and turned. He'd never seen Alex look lost before. He hated it.

Alex sat on the couch and waited for Corbin to sit down too, before he spoke. "Right now, I'm feeling like I took advantage of you. I'm your employer, and I feel like I pressured you into something you don't want, and I feel like absolute shit about it. If that's not the truth of what's going on here, I really want you to tell me. Please?" he added.

Corbin's pain turned to horror. That Alex could think he was at fault, when it was Corbin. When it was the curse. He shook his head. "It's not. That's not the truth at all."

"Then, please, Corbin. I know it's really hard for you to explain things sometimes. I know there are things you don't want to talk about. But *please,* will you try?"

Corbin tried. He opened his mouth and sorted through the words like stones, searching for the right one to start. And he didn't find it. He piled the words up and made a cairn and looked at it and knew that it was what lived inside him: a grave marking the place where something could have been. He felt a tear cut a track down his cheek.

"Corbin. Baby. Please. Let me help. This is fucking killing me." Alex's face was broken.

"That's what I'm afraid of!" Corbin yelled. "That it will kill you. That *I'll* kill you." He clasped both hands over his mouth to keep more stones from rolling out.

"What?"

He shook his head. Shook it and shook it until he was dizzy and his hair was blotting out his vision, like ink splashed across a page.

Then Alex's face was there, right in front of him. Alex didn't touch him, just looked at him.

"Listen. Whatever you're thinking or feeling. Whatever you're afraid of. I want you to tell me. I want you to tell me all of it. And I promise—Corbin, I *promise*—I won't leave. I won't stop caring about you. I won't think you're crazy. Whatever it is, I know it's real for you. I want to hear it."

Corbin groaned at the edge of command in his voice. He wanted to tell Alex everything. Wanted to disgorge a lifetime of secrets into his gentle, waiting hands.

Alex's eyes looked like home. His voice sounded like comfort and ease. His arms offered a haven.

"I want to," Corbin whispered. "I'm scared."

"I know," Alex said, and the certainty of it settled in Corbin's chest. He breathed in deeply to give it more space.

And then, with that certainty wrapped around his heart, holding him together, he spoke.

"I'm cursed. My family is cursed. Anyone we truly fall in love with—if they truly fall in love with us too . . . they die within a year."

The force of Corbin's heart slamming against his chest made him woozy, and blackness crept into his periphery.

"I can't touch you because I can't let the curse—the poison— get all over you. And I can't . . . I can't let us be together because then what if we . . . what if you . . ."

"What if we fell in love."

Corbin bit his lip and nodded. It sounded ridiculous, put so baldly. That Alex could love him. That Alex could ever choose someone wrong, like him.

"Did your aunts tell you about the curse?"

"Yeah. I've known since I was small. Aunt Hilda's man, Davey, died in the Marines, ten months after they fell in love. Aunt Jade's wife Maria was healthy until she died of a heart attack in her sleep, exactly six months after they got married. My father died of an aneurism a few months after I was conceived. And lots before them. Lots and lots. They all died. Everybody dies."

Alex's brows were drawn together, but it wasn't judgment or scorn, nor fear.

"I tried to break it," Corbin said, "I swear I really tried. What you said that day about bread tasting bitter . . . I went in early every day and I put all the bitterness, all the taint of the curse into the dough and then I burnt it. I thought maybe if I could get it out of me then I could finally . . . touch you. And then the oil. The miracle. I repeated it with the suf— Um. The doughnuts, and then I scorched them in the burning oil. And then I made good ones— better ones—for you. To, to reverse it. Sweetness for sweetness."

Alex was watching him intently, and he started to speak, but Corbin barreled ahead. "I watched so closely to try and see the signs—any signs that it was gone. Or that I was hurting you. And I tried to stay away. Alex. I tried so hard, I promise. I tried to stay away but I *couldn't*. Nothing had ever felt the way you felt, and the baking, and I just . . ." He hung his head. "I wanted it so badly," he whispered. "Even though I knew I was putting you in danger. I have to be alone. I know that. I've *always* known that. It felt so good for just a little while, though. Not to be alone."

Silence for what felt like forever, and Corbin couldn't look at Alex because the world would come crashing down. Finally, he felt Alex breathe in and out.

"The idea that if you ever love someone, if someone ever loves you, then they'll die," Alex said finally. "That's a really scary thought."

Corbin nodded, relieved that he understood the risk, the threat, even as his heart broke all over again. He curled up on the couch, knees to his chest, like a pill bug, and tried to make himself smaller. Tried to wrap himself around the breaking thing inside of him and hold the pieces together.

"Corbin." Alex's voice was painfully soft and Corbin squeezed his eyes shut against the resignation he heard there. "There's a problem, though."

Fear lanced through him, and he sat bolt upright. Could Alex already feel some of the poison working its way inward from when they kissed? "What. What is it. What's wrong."

"The problem is that even if you don't touch, even if you keep things back, even if you don't go out to dinner or to the movies, the feelings are still there. Because love doesn't live in kisses and flowers and first dates. It lives in your mind, in your heart. The problem is that I already love you."

Once, as a child, Corbin had been running upstairs and tripped on the rug. His head slammed into the bannister, and he fell to the ground, dazed, unable to make sense of the words of his aunts, looming over him.

He felt that way now. Alex was looking at him, Alex's mouth was moving. But everything after *love you* was a smear.

Then Alex was touching him, hands wrapped tight on his forearms, shaking him gently. The world came back into focus and

Corbin realized the smear was tears and it was his heart pounding so loudly in his ears that he couldn't hear anything else.

They stayed that way for a long time, Alex's hands on his arms, Alex's eyes searching his face. Long enough for Corbin to process what Alex had said before *love you*.

He realized that Alex was absolutely right. Love didn't live in kisses and first dates, but in your mind and heart. In the way a person could come to dwell there, uninvited, without ever touching you. In the way you thought about them and dreamed about them and wished about them, curse be damned—because though you could choose not to *act* on the feelings, the heart knows no logic but its own.

He grabbed at Alex, and at his movement, Alex came to him, pressed up close against him, fingers whisper-gentle but hands firm enough to pinion.

"Tell me," Alex said. "Tell me all of it."

"I didn't mean for it to happen," he whispered. "I was going to be alone. That was the plan. I—I've always known it. The curse is strong, stronger than anything. But then I saw you and you touched me, and it felt the way the aunts always described."

"How did it feel?" Alex's voice was a caress, his face all Corbin could see. Alex blotted out everything.

"Like the right thing. Only I didn't know what the right thing was. Like magic. Only I knew it wasn't. Like. Like everything was pointing me to you. Except why would it, because the curse." He shook his head.

This was what he'd been struggling to understand since the beginning. If they were cursed, why would the signs lead him to the person who might activate it? The only explanation was that the universe, instead of being indifferent, or kind, wished for him to suffer. And Corbin couldn't believe that. It wasn't what he'd ever known. The sky and the trees and the grass and the seasons—no, the universe wasn't vengeful. And Corbin was so small.

But if not, then . . . what?

"Why were you cursed?" Alex asked. "Did someone do it? I'm afraid I don't know that much about it."

"No. The curse was a wish for love that rebounded, formed itself around the wish, and twisted it inside out. You can't wish for things like that. You shouldn't wish at all, unless you know what you're doing."

"Your aunts told you that."

"Yes. But everyone knows that. You can't tinker around in the guts of the universe without knocking loose things you can't control."

"So with the baking, you were trying to siphon power from the curse little by little, instead of tinkering?" Corbin nodded. "That's smart. And you thought it worked, but then you just panicked a little. In case it hadn't?"

Corbin nodded again. "Do you believe me."

"I believe you absolutely," he said. "I believe that your aunts told you that, I believe that their lovers died. I believe that you've spent all these years alone. Thinking you'd always be alone. Which—" Alex sucked in a breath and dropped his forehead to Corbin's bent knees for a moment. "It breaks my heart, Corbin. But the curse itself? I'm not sure."

Corbin cocked his head in question.

"I've never thought about it before," Alex said. "I'm not sure the world I've experienced is a world where curses are quite as . . . rule-based as what you're describing." He looked thoughtful. "But I've certainly known people who had awful luck. They could do the same things I did and end up with far worse results. They were terribly unlucky in love. Things in their lives fell apart for seemingly no reason at all. And I've known people who were the opposite. Things just happened for them, without them even trying."

He took Corbin's hands and ran his thumbs over Corbin's knuckles.

"Who's to say what the difference is between bad luck and a curse, or good luck and a blessing? I really don't know."

From somewhere outside, a woodpecker knocked three times, then three more. A log cracked in half in the fire, sending sparks upward. And Corbin began to cry.

He had never been ashamed of crying, but it wasn't something he did in front of other people, either. Now, though, he looked into Alex's eyes and he cried.

Corbin found himself lifted in strong arms and settled onto Alex's lap as Alex sat back down. Alex's arms were tight around him, and he cried into Alex's chest. He cried for a long time.

He cried because reality had cracked open and inside had been another reality instead of nothing. He cried because no one had ever tried to understand him before, and Alex was trying. He cried because even if Alex didn't believe the curse was real, he believed it was true for Corbin. He cried because maybe, after a lifetime of living inside himself, he wouldn't have to be quite so alone.

He cried until he was exhausted. Then Alex picked him up and took him upstairs, shouldering open the door to his bedroom and striding inside like he had every right to be there. The air crackled and awoke, and Corbin could feel it even though his eyes were hot and swollen nearly shut.

"Go to sleep, baby," Alex murmured. "We'll figure everything out tomorrow."

The fingers of sleep clutched at him. But as Alex's warmth retreated, Corbin was wide awake. "No!" He reached for Alex, pulled his sleeve until he sat back down on the bed. "Don't leave. I'm—I'm afraid if you leave . . ."

"What?"

"You'll never come back."

Alex brushed his hair back. "I would never do that. But of course I'll stay. Do you want me to stay here with you, or downstairs?"

That Alex didn't even suggest he could sleep in Aunt Jade or Aunt Hilda's room sent Corbin's heart humming.

"Here," he whispered. If the curse was going to snap at Alex's heels and drag him down, surely it wouldn't be sleeping next to each other that would spring the trap? And Corbin didn't have the energy left to take every precaution.

Alex's smile was so soft, so intimate, that Corbin blushed and looked away.

Corbin started to undo his jeans, but then froze, hand on his zipper.

"You don't sleep in pajamas, huh?" Alex said with an appreciative smirk. "Well, I certainly don't mind. But maybe we want to go with underwear and T-shirts, just the first time."

Corbin nodded, relieved. He wanted to touch Alex, but the idea of all that skin . . . He shivered. It was too dangerous. Because of the curse, and for reasons he wasn't quite ready to process.

Alex opened his dresser and rummaged around, pulling out a clean white undershirt. "Here," he said. "Do you want me to turn around?"

Corbin flushed, but he shook his head. In his mind, Alex had watched him do this a hundred times. The idea of Alex's eyes on him now made his blood boil. He stripped off his wool sweater and the thermal shirt beneath it slowly, baring the skin of his stomach and chest to Alex's gaze. He pulled it over his head and dropped it next to the bed. He saw Alex swallow hard.

Next, his jeans, unzipped and slid off his hips, over his thighs, down his legs, and onto the floor. Then his socks.

Corbin sat on the bed, naked but for his underwear, and watched Alex watch him, searching the other man's face for some sign that he was pleased with what he saw.

Alex cleared his throat and adjusted his jeans, and when Corbin glanced down, he had all the sign he needed. He felt a surge of power at Alex's arousal. He pulled the clean white T-shirt over his head and shifted his bare legs under the covers. Alex never took his eyes off him.

"I don't think my shirts will fit you, but you can try."

Alex shook his head as if dazed, and went back into the

drawer. The sight of his hands touching all of Corbin's things settled comfortably in Corbin's stomach. Finally, he found a white tank undershirt. Looking back at Corbin, he unbuttoned his own shirt and let it fall to the floor. Then he undid his jeans and slid them off. He stood before Corbin, letting him look. It was only fair.

Corbin took in his broad chest and shoulders, large rib cage, and the rounded muscles of his arms and chest. The stretch of smooth skin and light brown hair in a trail down his stomach. He had thick, powerful thighs and a slight softness to his stomach that made Corbin want to rest his cheek there. He looked bigger without clothes, more immediate.

Once Alex pulled on the tank top, which stretched tight across his larger frame, Corbin reached out a hand to him and the air buzzed as they drew closer. The sudden *there*ness of Alex in his bed made Corbin shrink backward.

"I've never slept in the same bed as anyone," he said softly.

Alex looked like he was trying out things to say and rejecting each of them. Finally, he just leaned forward and kissed Corbin on the cheek, lips like the press of a thumb to the jam-filled cookies they'd made the week before. It made his heart race and his chest feel tight, and all he could think was *So much, this is so much, is it too much.*

"Are you all right?" Alex asked.

"Yes, I think so. I'm overwhelmed. This is a lot."

Then, at the pleading he could read in Alex's eyes, he tried to find the words. He'd never needed them before. Never had to explain himself, because the aunts had already known and others didn't care. Never had to make himself understood because Carbon and Jasmine and Lex and Finnian all understood already. Of course they did; they were him. And Wolf was Wolf, but Wolf didn't use words anyway.

"I always knew I'd be alone," Corbin said, trying to unravel the strands of thought that were tangled together, hovering just out of reach. "I always knew it, so I just made ways of keeping myself company. And that made it better. But now you're here, and you're . . . real, in a way they aren't quite."

"The people in your notebook. The ones you draw."

"Yes. I— Do you think that's weird."

"No, I think you're an amazing artist and it makes sense that art would be the medium you'd use to connect with people. Bakers bake, and writers write, and you draw. Each of us puts something of ourselves into our work."

Corbin blinked slowly. *That's right.*

"I don't understand why you're so different from everyone else," Corbin said. "I don't understand why you don't think I'm a freak. Why, even if you don't believe it's all real, you can see me so clearly."

"I don't know that I'm so different. Maybe a lot of people out there have their own Corbins. They're just not you." Corbin sat quietly, digesting that. "When I first moved to New York, I would stand at my apartment window and look out at the dozens of high rises I could see. Each one of them had hundreds of windows, and behind those were hundreds of people living completely singular lives, just like I was. And those were only the buildings I could see from my window. Across the city were thousands of buildings just like it. More, maybe. That's so many people. So many possibilities. So many ways of experiencing the world."

Alex shrugged and tucked Corbin's hair behind his ear.

"I don't really believe there's one destined soul mate for each person," he went on. "But I do think that with numbers like those, it's likely that no matter what you believe or who you are, there's someone out there—probably a lot of someones—who could see you clearly. Who could understand you, and care about you. Who could love you."

If Corbin hadn't already cried himself bone-dry downstairs, he thought he might cry at that. His throat tightened instead. "You really think so."

"Yeah, I do. You don't have to be all alone, Corbin. Not only because I'm here. I *am* here," he emphasized sternly, fingers possessive on Corbin's shoulder. "But you're going to have a whole life, and a lot of people are going to care for you. I know it."

"How," Corbin whispered.

Alex leaned in and kissed his mouth, soft and lingering.

"I just know, baby."

Chapter Sixteen

CORBIN'S DREAMS were up among the stars—pinpricks of light and swooping galaxies—and then they were in the dirt—seedlings shooting up in bloom, hair-delicate tangles of roots creeping down into the earth. Corbin's dreams were air and earth, a balance he rarely dreamed in.

As a child, Corbin had often watched Bethesda, a fluffy marmalade cat, fall asleep in a perfect circle of sun, her tail wound around her, and thought that she must be the most comfortable thing alive.

This morning, with the pale winter sun streaming through the open window, Corbin half awoke thinking of Bethesda, because he was held in the warm embrace of muscular arms, his head tucked under a stubbly chin, and his limbs splayed on the bed, making him feel as if he'd melted. His head was fuzzy and his breath even and he made a sound in his throat as if he were trying to purr.

The arms around him tightened and he came awake.

Alex Alex Alex.

Alex nuzzled his hair and made a low grumbling sound before he said, "Mmm, good morning."

Corbin squeezed his eyes shut and then opened them again to double check.

"Are you real."

He felt Alex press against every part of him, turning him so they faced each other.

"Yeah, I'm real."

Alex's face was relaxed from sleep, his eyes heavy-lidded, his hair mussed, his lips slightly chapped. He slung an arm over

Corbin's waist and dragged him in as close as they'd been spooned before.

"You're everywhere," Corbin murmured, surprised, and he felt Alex's groan rumble through his chest.

"Yeah, well. I'm right where I want to be."

He traced Corbin's mouth with his fingertip, and Corbin let his eyes flutter shut.

He must have slipped back into sleep, because the next thing he knew, he woke with his head on Alex's chest and his arm flung over Alex's stomach.

"You awake?"

Corbin muffled a noise in Alex's shoulder then slowly opened his eyes. It was sunny outside and he was perfectly warm with Alex's heat around him.

He sat bolt upright. "We're late! What time is it."

"It's okay, Hector's going to work today."

"I'm supposed to work today." Shades of all the jobs he'd been fired from played in his mind. They were always worse than the ones he'd simply stopped going to because the signs had told him he should.

Alex grasped his shoulders as he tried to roll out of bed.

"Hey. We've still got a lot to figure out. Please, take today off."

"I— You want me to," he asked. He wanted Alex to say yes, wanted to stay here, warm and held.

"I want you to," Alex said, and that made it all right.

Corbin nodded and let himself be drawn back into bed.

"I have a lot of questions," Alex said. "I don't want to over-whelm you, or be intrusive. I know sometimes I can seem like I'm giving an order or something when I'm really asking. Something about my voice, I guess. People have always said it."

Corbin swallowed around a lump in his throat and looked down at the duvet, suddenly intensely aware of Alex's eyes on him.

"Unless . . ." Alex's voice took on an edge. He lifted up on one elbow so he was looking down at Corbin, but kept his expression neutral. "You like when I'm giving orders. You like when I overwhelm you."

Corbin blinked rapidly, all the blood rushing from his head.

"You do," Alex said.

Corbin squeezed his eyes shut. It was too much. It was too much of everything he'd always wanted at once, and he felt like he might fly to pieces.

"Corbin, open your eyes." Alex infused his voice with command and Corbin opened his eyes. "It's okay. That's very good to know. We'll come back to that in a bit."

Alex went downstairs in his underwear to make coffee, and Corbin drifted. He closed his eyes and sought other signs. Smells and sounds were more trustworthy than sights at moments like these.

But outside his window things were still, sounds muffled, smells blank. He walked to the window, shivering, and looked out onto a world of white. The sun shone, but the ground and trees and Alex's car were blanketed in a foot of snow.

A fresh snowfall is a clean slate, perfect for trading truths.

An arm wrapped around his stomach and he startled, but Alex caught him and steadied him.

"Well, hello, Michigan," Alex said, breath ruffling Corbin's hair.

"It's so beautiful."

They got back into bed and Alex pressed a mug of coffee into his hand. Corbin sipped, the earthy bitterness of the coffee a welcome jolt back into reality.

"You have questions," he said.

Alex studied him, then ran a hand through his hair. "You know what? Don't worry. I got ahead of myself. We don't have to figure everything out today. We have plenty of time. Let's just talk, okay?"

Corbin nodded. He wasn't sure if he felt relieved to be off the hook, or disappointed not to have everything dragged out of him, once and for all.

"You said that you started drawing your friends in your notebook because they made you feel less alone." Corbin nodded. "Did you ever have other friends? Real-life friends. Or lovers?"

"Is this just talking. It feels like questions."

"Well, talking can include questions," Alex said sheepishly. Corbin rolled his eyes.

"Not really. I had a couple friends when I was small. I'd see them in the park or running around in the woods. But when we got a little older and they knew where I lived . . . People thought the aunts were . . ." *Freaks, witches, sorcerers, devils, criminals.* "Frightening."

"Why?" Alex asked gently.

"Because they seemed a little scary to kids, I guess. They were twins and they would dress the same. But Aunt Jade's mouth was all twisted because of a scar, and when she smiled, it looked wrong. Aunt Hilda didn't like to make eye contact. She saw their futures when she looked into their eyes, and she didn't want to see."

"And did you ever have lovers?"

Corbin felt the blood rush into his ears again, oceanic and deafening.

"I— No, I— Not exactly."

"Can you tell me more?" Alex slid a hand to his shoulder and squeezed, and Corbin took a gulp of his coffee too quickly and coughed.

"A couple of times people asked me. Men. Asked me. But I didn't want them. I didn't want them to touch me."

The thin, dark-haired man sitting with his wife outside the movie theater, holding their infant daughter. The man's eyes raking over Corbin's face and body. The lust there. Inside, in the bathroom, Corbin washing his hands and the man coming in, closing the door behind him. Coming up so close Corbin could smell him—fabric softener, and milk, and shame. *Want to?* And Corbin saying *No.* Pushing open the door and walking outside into the sunlight because the dark of the movie theater left too much space for wondering.

"You said 'not exactly.'" Alex took his hand. "What does that mean?"

"I don't know if I should tell you. I don't know if it's the kind of thing that people talk about."

"I want to know everything."

Corbin swallowed hard. "I have sex . . . with myself. But I, um. One of the people I draw in my notebook. Finnian. He— We have sex. I imagine that he tells me what to do, and then I do it."

Alex's hand tightened on his shoulder.

"Do you do it that way because you like him telling you what to do?"

"Yes. It's just what I've always imagined. I— He sits there." He pointed to the bed where Alex was sitting. "And he tells me how to, um. How to touch myself. What to do. When to . . ."

"When to come?" Alex's voice was low, and Corbin darted a glance at Alex's lap. His underwear was bulging.

Corbin nodded. "Is that . . . Do you think that's strange."

"I think that's outrageously hot." Alex leaned closer. "How does he play with you, Corbin? What does he make you do?"

Corbin couldn't quite get a full breath. "It depends. Sometimes he makes it take a long time, makes me touch myself softly until I'm . . ."

"Begging," Alex growled.

"Yeah. Sometimes he has me, um . . ."

"Does he have you fuck yourself, baby? With your fingers or with a toy?"

A broken whimper escaped from Corbin's throat. "Yes," he whispered.

"Do you like it when he makes you fuck yourself?" Alex's voice was low and hypnotic and scraped over Corbin's skin.

"Yes," he gasped.

"What do you think about while he's making you fuck yourself open? Do you imagine he's fucking you?"

Corbin's heart was pounding so fast he was lightheaded, and beneath the covers, he was rock hard.

"No, I— Oh god. I . . . I don't want to tell you."

"Why?"

"Because I'm afraid it's weird. Everything about me is weird. What if I do this weird too and I don't know it."

Alex put his hand on Corbin's chest, fingers spread and palm pressed against his heart. He pushed a little, and Alex fell back on the bed.

"I want you to imagine that there's no such thing as weird. Do you know what I want most?" Corbin listened harder than he'd ever listened to anything. "I want to know *everything*. Do you understand? I want to know everything you fantasize about, everything that makes you feel good, everything you want. There's nothing you could say that would make me think you were doing this wrong. Do you believe me?"

He believed that Alex meant it, but he didn't quite believe it could be true. *That's just what Alex said last night.*

"I'll try."

For that he got a kiss on the cheek, and Alex moved closer, propping himself on his side next to Corbin. "Tell me what you imagine when he's making you fuck yourself. Tell me what you think about."

Corbin closed his eyes. "I— Sometimes I imagine that my hand can reach all the way inside me. That my fingers grow like tree roots all through me, twine around my heart and reach up into my throat and . . . take me over from the inside."

Alex whispered, "Jesus," and Corbin squeezed his eyes tighter shut. "What else?"

"The same thing when I imagine it's a person. He has me use a toy . . . a vibrator or— And I imagine . . ."

"You imagine it's a cock inside you? Deep inside you, filling you up?"

Corbin whimpered and nodded. "Yes, and—and it expands

until it's everywhere and I can't breathe and I can't think and it's just *that* inside me and it doesn't ever stop."

"Corbin, fuck, what else?"

"I, lately, well. It turned into you." He said the last sentence in a whisper, but he knew Alex heard because he groaned and dropped his forehead to Corbin's shoulder.

"Open your eyes."

Corbin blinked his eyes open.

"That's the hottest thing I've ever heard in my life. I can't even tell you how turned on I am right now."

"Me too."

"Is it only a fantasy? Or do you want me to fuck you? I'll do anything you want. Or we can do nothing."

Corbin's head was spinning. Did he want Alex to fuck him? The thought alone practically made him spin apart with desire. But when he thought about Alex that close to him—*inside of him*—what if the curse . . . what if it *did* something to them. Struck them dead or rebounded, the way curses do, and turned love to hate, desire to disgust? Such things had been known to happen with curses.

The thoughts ricocheted around Corbin's mind until he realized minutes had gone by and he hadn't answered Alex.

Suddenly, he saw a workaround.

"I do want that. So much. But maybe not quite yet. What if . . . would you want to . . . do what Finnian does?"

He risked a glance at Alex. Alex's eyes closed for a moment, and when they opened, Alex looked like he was about to consume him.

"Would I want to order you around and tell you how to touch yourself while I watch? *Fuck yes.*"

Corbin relaxed. "I've imagined it."

"You've imagined me telling you how to fuck yourself?" Alex ran a hand over his jaw. "That's . . . amazing. That's amazing. You'll have to let me know if I can take any pointers from your fantasy version of me."

"No. I want real you."

"Okay, baby." Alex leaned in and kissed his mouth. "I guess I can't touch you in this scenario, huh."

"No, you can't."

"Not at all?" Alex kissed the pulse in Corbin's neck, and Corbin felt engulfed by a cloud of lust. Alex sucked at the spot and Corbin gasped, then pushed him away.

"You—you can't. That's how it works."

Alex's smile was wicked as he leaned back, but his eyes lingered on Corbin's neck, clearly making plans for when he was allowed to touch.

"What am I working with here?"

Corbin opened the drawer of the bedside table and Alex looked through the dildos, vibrators, plugs, and beads.

"Oh, Corbin," he murmured, half threat and half worship, and suddenly Corbin was shaking with need. Alex wasn't even touching him, but he could feel sensation zinging through his body, like electricity was jumping from nerve ending to nerve ending.

"Tell me what you don't want me to have you do."

He couldn't imagine a single thing he wouldn't do if Alex asked him to.

"Nothing. I don't know. Nothing."

Alex nodded. "We'll talk about it later, okay? You just let me know if there's something you don't like. Will you?"

"Yeah."

"Good. Pull the bedcovers down. I want to see you."

Corbin pulled the blanket down, his skin heating under Alex's gaze. Alex watched him for a long time. It wasn't the way Finnian had looked at him. Finnian had regarded him as if he were looking in a mirror. Alex stared as if he wanted to climb inside.

"God, you're beautiful. Close your eyes if you want. Let your mind go wherever it wants to go."

At that, Corbin knew it would be all right, and he let his eyes drift shut.

"Lift up your shirt and touch your stomach." For a moment Corbin paused, because it was the way Finnian so often started. Then he smiled. Finnian had prepared him for this, even if he hadn't known it. Another sign pointing straight at Alex.

Corbin slid his palm to the sensitive skin of his belly and shivered at his own touch. It was more intense with Alex watching, like a feedback loop of pleasure. Him touching himself, Alex watching him touch himself, feeling Alex watching him.

"Touch your nipples. Pinch them if you want to. Let me see."

Corbin pinched his nipples, flinching away from his fingers and then pressing into them as the pain and pleasure crested and ebbed. As the sensations suffused his skin, his mind spiraled off.

He found himself by the ocean, sand rough beneath his shoulder blades. Abrasive. He could hear the crash of the waves, and the sun shone brightly overhead. Alex was the sun, he realized, his warm regard falling over every inch of his skin.

"Alex," he whispered. "I feel you."

"Good. I'm right here. Everything you feel, that comes from me. I want to make you feel good. Do you want that?"

"Yes. Please."

Under Alex's command, Corbin touched himself. Fingertips running over his throat and trailing down his stomach and hips and thighs was sand blowing around him. Featherlight touches behind his knees and in the crooks of his elbows were the ocean lapping at him. A hand tangled in his hair, tugging gently, was seaweed wrapping around him to hold him in place.

Corbin panted, every inch of his skin sensitized by sand and sea and sun.

"Do you know how hard you are already? You're leaking for me, Corbin. Run a finger over the tip of your dick and feel how wet you are."

"Ohh," Corbin moaned, and shuddered with the contact. He rubbed small circles over the tip of his leaking erection, shuddering with pleasure.

"Stroke yourself. Very slowly."

Corbin's hand on himself was the ocean, collecting itself into the instrument of his pleasure. Drag of the tides and pull of the waves controlled his strokes, his body sinking into the wet sand like it could cover him, envelop him.

Corbin's moans were the calls of sea birds and the groan of creaking ships. The water that stroked him was blood-hot and full up with salt, and when Alex told him to stop, he could feel the sun burning his face, the bright-red flush spreading down his chest and to his stomach and thighs like sunburn.

"Here, take this." Something was pressed into his hand, hard and slick. The vibrator. His favorite. Somehow Alex had known.

"I want you to turn that on and tease your hole with it," the sun whispered low in his ear. Sun speaking to sand and water. Corbin turned it on and it was the vibrations of sand when the ground shook with thunder. It woke up every nerve, teased his muscles until he felt the gentle waves of it echoing inside.

"Do you want it inside?" the sun asked.

"Oh god, please, please, please," Corbin chanted. Every pulse of vibration was a wave hitting the shore.

"Spread your legs for me." As Corbin did, he felt more lube swiped onto the vibrator. "Now, slowly. Press it inside."

As the length of it breached him, the vibrations intensified. This was a storm at sea, the crash and shatter of water made solid enough to bruise. He pressed it inside, deeper, deeper, until he felt the vibrations everywhere.

"Move it so it feels good," Alex said. "I want to watch you fall apart."

Corbin squirmed in the sand, the soles of his feet pressing down, his hips pressing up, then back, thighs tensing and releasing. He pulsed the vibrations over his prostate and a gulf opened up inside of him. This was how the ocean got in. Here, where he shook himself apart. A wave curled to a wicked point and blasted up through him, stroking every inch.

Distantly, Corbin heard desperate sounds, broken sounds, and realized they weren't the screeching of a low flying gull, but his own needy moans as the pleasure overwhelmed him.

He formed them into sense and what they formed was "Alex, Alex, Alex."

"You're safe. Tell me where you are. Tell me what you feel."

"I'm— Oh god— The ocean is inside me. You're the sun. No, now the moon because the moon controls the tides, and so you make the waves. And the waves make me feel everything." Corbin gasped as the sea moved deeper inside him, pressing further against the shore.

"What else, baby?"

"It—it's so deep. I can feel the way it shakes apart and rolls back together and—oh god, oh god, I— Every time it comes back together it's farther inside me."

"Where is it now?" Alex purred.

"It . . . I don't—it's all the way inside my—my ass and pressing up into my stomach. The ocean can go anywhere, it never stops. It —it—*fuck* mmmm— I can't, I don't know what it will do."

"Turn it up," Alex whispered.

And then the sea took him apart. It slammed through him and shook him to pieces like a shell.

"It's in my chest," Corbin gasped. "It wants to run *through* me." Corbin felt his cock burn, swollen and hot, a brand against his stomach on the very edge of erupting. "Oh god, Alex, please, can I—"

He felt Alex's breath on his neck. "Not yet. Not yet. Just a little while longer."

Corbin whined as the waves twisted inside him and his hips rocked as he was fucked straight through. His entire body was shaking with the need for release, cradled in the sand, flooded by the ocean, scraped to prickles by the wind.

"I need— Please, please, please," Corbin begged, not sure if he was begging for release or annihilation, or if they were one and the same.

The sand shifted beside him and he felt Alex close.

"Alex— Oh Alex, it's in my throat," he whispered, then his voice was smothered by salty spray.

"Let the sea take you where it wants," Alex whispered. Then Corbin felt a hand on his throat, outside, where the sea pulsed beneath. Alex squeezed gently and Corbin shuddered and gasped. Pressure outside and pressure inside, until he was caught between the waves like driftwood. Broken sounds choked out of him and he writhed on the sand.

"Come for me now."

A finger of seaweed tapped at the tip of his aching cock, slid inside, then wrapped itself around the head, squeezing, and Corbin was gone.

The wave slammed through him, opening him up to a force of pleasure as ancient and inexorable as the tides. He seized with it, pulse after pulse erupting from him, wave after wave inside him, squeeze after squeeze around him. He was left on the beach, wrung dry, his limbs shaking and jerking with lingering jolts. He saw only blackness, and he heard only the crash of the waves, and in his mouth was blood salt heat.

Then the sun eclipsed him, smothered him, and took his mouth in a burning kiss. A hand pressed the ocean back inside of him for a final spray of vibration, and he was turned inside out, heaving with another great rip of pleasure that tore through him as the sun made itself known.

Slowly, the sea receded. The beach was peaceful, the sun a warm glow. Every limb was relaxed, his muscles melted. Soft kisses, like butterflies, landed over his cheeks, and he blinked his eyes open.

He was in his bed, skin flushed, head spinning, Alex looking at him like he was watching something incredible.

They blinked at one another for a few seconds.

"You touched me," Corbin said, but it came out in a rasp.

"I cheated," Alex said, his own voice rough too. "I actually couldn't stop myself. I tried."

Corbin smiled weakly. "The sun touched me."

"What?"

"Was it— Did you like— Was that okay," Corbin asked.

Alex's eyes burned. "That was the sexiest fucking thing I've ever experienced." He gestured at his crotch, and Corbin's eyes widened to see the soaked front of his underwear. It made him burn with a different kind of heat.

He reached out a tentative hand, and Alex slid flush against him.

"You were so gorgeous," he murmured. "And your mind. It's beautiful." Alex brushed his hair back. "You remake the world a hundred times a day."

Chapter Seventeen

CORBIN RAN a finger up Alex's arm, which was flung over his legs. They were sitting on the living room rug, leaning against the couch, in front of the fire. They'd been there nearly all day, and Corbin didn't think he'd ever talked so much at one time in his life. His voice was growing hoarse from overuse, but the words were coming more and more easily.

They'd talked about Alex's father, and what Corbin remembered of his mother. About what other kinds of signs Corbin saw and what other stories his aunts had told him. About how Alex had met Gareth, and the places he'd traveled. About Corbin's dreams and his notebooks.

Corbin felt like a rusted lock that had finally found its key.

"When you left school and didn't come back, was it only because your aunts died? Or because of that guidance counselor?"

"After my aunts died, I lost time. But there was also no reason to go back. It was them who would get in trouble for not sending me to school."

"Didn't the school try and contact you?"

"I told them I moved to live with family." Corbin shrugged. "Wasn't very hard. It was a big school."

"I remember when you left because people told wild stories about it."

Corbin leaned back against Alex's shoulder. He could imagine the kinds of tales people would have spun.

The snow hadn't melted and more had fallen throughout the day. Now, as the sun began to set, the white ground began to glow an eerie blue. There was a whine from outside and Corbin pulled himself up.

"Wolf," he whispered into the cold. Wolf, Stick, and Dreidel were bounding toward him, running around each other with the joy of companionship and snow.

"Finally cold enough to come inside," he asked Wolf, but Wolf just pawed at the snow and barked once. Stick and Dreidel trooped inside, leaving wet paw prints on the wood. "You sure."

Wolf barked once more, and settled in next to the door, posture expectant, blue eyes watching Corbin.

"I think I might have broken the curse," Corbin whispered into Wolf's tufted ear. "I might get to keep Alex. Maybe."

Wolf leaned his head against Corbin, nuzzling at him. Corbin could feel the animal's warm, quiet satisfaction on his behalf.

FOR THE NEXT FEW DAYS, Corbin couldn't concentrate at work. Every time Alex came near him, the sugar turned to salt, the flour to cornstarch. When Alex pressed a furtive kiss to his hair, the egg whites curdled. When Alex slung an arm around his shoulders and pulled him close, the chocolate seized. All he could think about was Alex in his bed the morning after the Chanukah dinner, and what it would be like when he got Alex in his bed again.

Gareth came into the kitchen at lunchtime to drop off Alex's car keys, and stood in the doorway staring at them.

"Whoa. The vibe in here is so intense I feel like I might get pregnant if I stay. Um, Alex, is it cool if maybe I have the house to myself tonight?"

Alex raised an eyebrow.

"Corbin, that means he'd have to stay with you," Gareth said when Alex remained silent.

"You can stay with me," Corbin said. His heart started

pounding at thoughts of what might happen and the butter he was creaming melted.

Once Gareth left, Alex put a hand on his shoulder. "I don't have to stay if you don't want. That was an ill-advised attempt on Gareth's part to play wingman."

Corbin didn't know what that meant, but he was already flushing at how badly he wished Alex would close the space between them and kiss him.

"Do you know how you're looking at me right now?" Alex growled. "It's making me pretty sure you're okay with me staying over."

"I want you to kiss me," Corbin said, and watched Alex's eyes darken.

"You can kiss me, you know."

"I know. But I want you to kiss me."

"Your wish is my command," Alex murmured.

The kiss started sweetly, Alex leaning close and cupping Corbin's cheek. But when Corbin touched his tongue to Alex's, they found themselves crushed together, mouths moving desperately.

Corbin pulled away first. He could smell the bread in the oven starting to burn with the added heat.

"Are we almost done," Corbin asked. They needed to burn off some of the tension between them or they'd ruin everything in the kitchen.

"I'll never be done with you," Alex said, looking almost shocked at his own words.

"With work, I mean. We're messing things up. Everything's going all weird."

"What does that mean?"

"We're melting the butter and burning the bread."

Alex grinned at him and ran a thumb over his lips. "I hear you. Let me get the last batch of cookies and bread out and we'll go."

In the car, Corbin was quiet. Since they'd spent the night

together, he'd watched Alex intently to make sure that he didn't see any evidence of the curse wreaking havoc. But Alex had seemed as confident and calm as ever. He'd kissed Corbin hello and goodbye, and smiled at him. He'd grabbed him by the elbow when he'd tripped, and told him his maple scones were perfect.

But he hadn't come back to Corbin's house. And Corbin didn't know why. Moreover, Corbin didn't know if Alex's behavior was how such things normally went or not.

"Alex," he said as he let them inside. "What happens next." He'd been looking for signs but none had appeared. Without their guidance, he felt lost, like one of his senses was missing.

"Are you hungry? I could make dinner. Or we could order something."

"No. *Next*. How do we know what happens."

"What happens next in our relationship?"

Alex combed his fingers through Corbin's hair and it shot a shivers down his spine. Corbin nodded and Alex pulled him down onto the couch.

"Anything we want."

Corbin cocked his head. "Something still feels unsettled. It's felt strange all day. The last few days. Since . . . You know."

"Since we spent the night together, declared our love for each other, confessed our secrets, had the greatest sex ever, and hung out all day talking?"

Corbin choked on a laugh. "Yeah."

"Yeah, baby. The earth shifted that day. It's going to take a little while to be on an even keel again."

"What do you mean."

"I mean, it was really intense, really intimate. I've been feeling a little raw myself."

"You have." Alex nodded and Corbin felt better. "That's how I feel sometimes. Like my skin has been stripped off and I'm just nerves being scraped by everything."

Alex stroked the back of his neck softly. "Does anything help?"

"I go away with Carbon and Lex and Jasmine and Finnian. Or

I go in the woods with Wolf. In the summer, sometimes I'll work in the garden. My aunts always grew all our vegetables, but a lot of them died."

"Maybe this summer Gareth could help you get it back up and running. His family had a huge garden growing up and he really missed it in New York. I bet he'd love to help."

Corbin nodded, his mind wandering to Gareth and what he knew about him. "Is he all right. He seemed so . . . bruised when he first got here."

"I'm not sure. He left New York to get away from his husband, Paul. And I keep asking him if Paul's called him, but he won't tell me. It's good he's here now, but I worry he might feel drawn back there."

Corbin hesitated before he spoke. "Are you going to be here now. To stay."

The air around them jangled, alive with tension.

"I don't think I meant to at first. When my mom gave me the coffee shop, I imagined I'd stay for a year or two, relax, get my head together, sell it at a profit and give my mom the money, and then go. But after I met you, I didn't feel that way anymore." He grasped Corbin's hands.

Corbin didn't think he'd ever held hands with anyone before. Their fingers were braided together like the challahs they had made, Alex's palm a warm rasp against his own.

"Now, I can't think of anywhere I'd rather be than here, with you. I don't know what your plans are, but—"

Corbin launched himself at Alex and kissed him with everything he had.

As they kissed, the air around them settled, the storm allayed. Until now, Corbin hadn't realized what would be the thing to set his quaking nerves to rights, to make the jangled, *wrong* feeling he'd been mired in the last few days recede. Hadn't known the jittery uncertainty was the idea that maybe they had broken the curse . . . and Alex might leave anyway.

Corbin kissed down Alex's jaw to his neck, and climbed into his lap, holding on to him.

Alex *mmm*ed, then leaned back. "Is that yes, you want me to stay?"

"*Yes.*"

Alex twined his fingers into Corbin's hair and studied his face. "What *are* your plans? What do you want to do going forward?"

Corbin chewed on his lip. He'd never made any plans. Never thought of his jobs as anything more than money to buy groceries or pay the water bill. He'd never dared to dream of anything because he hadn't known how. Now, suddenly, he felt as if the future yawned open before him like a grassy field. It was all *there*, wide swathes of it, all at once rather than revealing itself pace by pace as he walked forward.

No one had ever asked him what he wanted. He'd never asked himself.

"I want . . . to have something that's mine."

The words left his mouth and shimmered in front of his lips like soap bubbles, as shining with promise and as delicate.

"I've never had that. This house was my aunts', and everything in it. My friends in my notebooks . . . they're a part of me—Parts of me. The dogs belong to themselves. I don't know what, but something."

"You'll figure it out," Alex said, and Corbin believed him.

"Alex." Corbin bit at his nails. "I still want to spend time with them. With Carbon and . . . everyone."

"Of course," Alex said. "They're your friends."

Alex didn't mention Finnian and what they'd done together. Corbin flushed and smiled as thoughts of Finnian turned into thoughts of Alex, and everything they hadn't yet done.

"Alex."

"God, I love the way you say my name."

Corbin looked into Alex's face, all clean lines and generous mouth and those eyes that saw him as no one ever had. "I want you to fuck me."

Heat flooded Alex's eyes and his fingers tightened almost painfully around Corbin's.

Then Corbin found himself crushed to Alex's chest, his mouth taken in a bruising kiss. Alex's tongue stroked against his lips and he opened his mouth to let him in. They kissed and kissed until they were both panting and grinding together.

Finally, Alex broke the kiss and stared, mouth swollen and red as a cherry.

"Let's go upstairs."

Corbin nodded and stumbled to his feet, heart racing. As soon as they got to his room, Alex was on him, hands running up his back, mouth on his neck. They tumbled to the bed and Corbin pulled Alex on top of him, wanting to feel his solid weight everywhere.

He tilted up his chin and Alex kissed him slow and deep, braced on his forearms on the bed. Corbin sank into the kiss and he pulled at Alex's shoulders to press them even more tightly together.

"I want you to crush me."

Alex stopped holding himself up, lay full out on Corbin and wound his arms around him.

"Yes, please. Everywhere."

Alex squeezed him so tight he couldn't move at all, and almost couldn't breathe, then he began to lick at his neck. Alex licked and sucked at Corbin's pulse point, and waves of heat rolled through him. Alex bit lightly at the curve where neck met shoulder and the scrape of his teeth was electrifying. He kissed Corbin's throat, up over his jaw and behind his ear, and Corbin's hips thrust up in arousal, but he couldn't move.

Corbin dragged in a breath. "Kiss me, please kiss me." Alex kissed him, devouring his mouth, sucking on his tongue and nipping at his lips until Corbin was so hot he felt feverish. He shifted his legs out from under Alex's heavy weight and wrapped them around Alex, rubbing them together.

Alex eased up enough to align them perfectly, then thrust their hips together. Bolts of pleasure shot up Corbin's spine and he felt himself thrusting and thrusting, seeking that sensation again.

When Alex moved away, Corbin whimpered and grabbed for him, not wanting to lose the contact for a moment. Alex stripped them both quickly, never breaking eye contact as Corbin panted. Alex opened the bedside drawer and put the lube on the table, then he paused.

"You don't have any condoms, do you?" Corbin shook his head. "I got tested right after I moved here, and I haven't been with anyone else since then. We can wait if you want, though."

"No, I don't want to wait. I want . . ." Corbin had never thought about this part, precisely, but what he wanted was so clear, suddenly. "I need to feel you, please. I want you like that."

"Fuck, me too," Alex ground out.

Alex spread Corbin's legs with thumbs on his hips and kissed and sucked the join of his thigh. He sucked up blooms of blood under the pale, untouched skin and Corbin felt the bursting of each blood vessel, he was so attuned to Alex's mouth on his flesh. Alex scraped stubble against the insides of Corbin's thighs where he'd scratched himself in days gone by, but this was a rasping pleasure he had never felt.

"Yes, please," Corbin gasped, and Alex rubbed his cheek over the delicate skin until it pinked. When Alex's mouth closed over his cock, Corbin nearly flew off the bed. He felt like his very arousal itself was being swallowed by a vortex, sucking him inexorably into a black hole. Pull after pull of pleasure left him wrecked on the bed as he quivered toward an explosion.

Then it all stopped and Corbin lay shaking, his body on fire.

"*Alex*," he insisted, and Alex groaned out, "Fuck, please, I need to be inside you," and Corbin said, "*Yes, yes, yes.*"

Slick fingers slid inside him, and Corbin thought absently that they didn't feel like his own at all. The way they moved, the size of them and the pressure, the unpredictability, it was all so different that it seemed an entirely other sensation.

Then he lost the ability to catalogue difference because Alex was kissing him and fucking him with his fingers and he was so overwhelmed by the onslaught of sensation that he kept thinking he was orgasming, but when he looked down his cock stood, hard and swollen and leaking against his stomach.

"You, you, you," Corbin begged, tugging at Alex's wrist. Alex's fingers slid out of him and he slicked himself up, breathing shallowly.

He kissed Corbin's lips and bumped their foreheads together. "I do love you," he murmured in wonder. "I really do."

Corbin tried to say it back, because incantations were all about repetition, but he found his heart had taken up residence in his throat and all he could do was nod and hope his eyes spoke for him. He thought Alex understood.

"I hope if your hot-as-fuck brain goes someplace amazing you'll tell me about it," Alex said with a smile, and Corbin closed his eyes, peace washing over him.

Corbin's fantasies of a man fucking him had so often been oceans and planets and stars. As Alex pressed inside of him it was earth. The hot honesty of ground and flesh and rock. Alex's hips pressed flush against Corbin's and he paused, completely inside. He leaned forward slowly and pressed a kiss to Corbin's mouth. They stayed that way for a moment, lips touching, chests touching, bodies interlocked. To Corbin, it felt like time stopped.

Alex slid forward on his knees and slung Corbin's legs over his shoulders, and Corbin closed his eyes and let himself feel everything. The flesh inside him swelled impossibly large, pressing against muscle. As Alex began to move in deep, heavy thrusts, Corbin started to shake. Each stroke of Alex's cock teased him open, and he squeezed himself tight around it until Alex groaned and swore.

As the thrusts grew harder and more powerful, Corbin lost himself. He clutched at Alex's shoulders because he thought otherwise he might be pounded to pieces that would fly apart in all directions. His ass, his cock, his stomach, his thighs, all of it was one reverberation of pleasure as Alex moved, stroking over his prostate until he felt liquefied and mad with pleasure.

Then it happened. He could feel it. Alex's cock swelled and grew and broke through something inside him, pressing deep, deep, like the tree roots, deep, like the ocean waves, deep, up through into his stomach. Still, Alex moved, hot and slick like he'd been formed of clay to fit perfectly inside. Corbin cried out, and that great pressure moved deeper still. Into his chest where he felt it in his heart and all through his lungs, as if his every breath would be Alex.

He pulled Alex down so he could feel even more of his weight, so it was Alex all around him and Alex all inside him, taking over every empty space and churning it all to throbs of pleasure.

"Alex, Alex, Alex," he chanted, "you're so deep in me, you're everywhere, you're the earth," and Alex's groan was a desperate thing pulled from him like sucking poison.

In his throat now, and if he swallowed he knew he would be swallowing around Alex, and his ears were full, his nose, his mouth, and then Corbin smiled with the brightness of ten thousand suns because he was free. He couldn't tell Alex because he couldn't speak, he was so perfectly full of him.

Fuck, baby, and *Oh god,* and their moans rose together, and Alex's hand closed around Corbin's swollen erection and he was coming in great gasping screams of joy, each faraway piece of him exploding.

When Alex cried out his pleasure, Corbin felt a blast of heat inside him that seared him everywhere. Burning in his ass, up in his guts, his heart and lungs, and lingering in his throat. He could taste the clay of Alex, mineral and elemental.

Seconds, minutes, hours, millennia, and Corbin came back to himself. Alex tried to pull out, and Corbin wrapped arms and legs around him so he couldn't move. He needed to feel this just a little while longer.

Alex was stroking his face and the curve of his thigh and

kissing him softly, whispering things Corbin couldn't understand, but he felt them anyway.

Finally, they separated and lay facing each other, noses nearly touching.

"You're incredible," Alex said, but Corbin knew he hadn't done anything.

He shook his head and kissed Alex. "You were everywhere," he whispered.

A shudder ran through Alex. "You don't know what it does to me to hear you say that." But Corbin thought he did know.

"Alex."

"Yeah, baby."

"I want to get you something for Chanukah. It's not over, is it." Corbin wasn't great with time.

"Nope, two more nights." He ran his palm up and down Corbin's side under the covers. "You want to know what I really want?"

"Yes."

"I really want to stay here with you for the next two days, and walk through the woods with you, and eat with you. I want to take a shower with you, and cook eggs with you. And I want to do this about ten more times." He smiled, a soft sincere smile.

"I want that," Corbin said, shifting closer. "Is that a Chanukah present."

"It's the best present I can possibly imagine. And you never know. Maybe some Chanukah magic will shine down on us, and you'll know for sure that the curse is broken."

"I know you're teasing me, but . . . you did say magic was the possibility of something that seemed otherwise impossible. Well . . . This all seems pretty impossible to me. You. Us. This."

Corbin pressed his face into Alex's neck and breathed in his smell. Freshly turned earth, heavy clay, salt, and the sweet hint of almonds.

As Alex's hand came around him, squeezing the back of his neck, Corbin sighed in pleasure.

Something deep inside him settled into an unfamiliar pattern of knowledge.

Love was a curse. No love was a curse.

Solitude was a cure. Solitude was a torment.

Distance was safety. Distance was crushing.

There was more in the world than he'd ever been told. And there was less.

And here he lay, tangled up with the person he was in love with, for better or for worse. If the curse wasn't broken, it was too late. The trap had already been sprung.

But if it *was* broken. If he could have a future. With Alex, and with this version of himself that could see more than signs. Then he *wanted* it. He wanted to fall asleep with Alex each night, knowing that there would be a morning to wake up to with him. And a morning after that. And enough mornings that they would hang together into something he could call a life.

He was nearly breathless with how much he wanted it.

"Maybe it is magic," Alex murmured sleepily into his hair. "Feels perfect to me."

Corbin breathed deeply as he drifted off to sleep in Alex's arms. Earth from Alex and sea from himself. Fire between them. Outside, winter air gusting fresh snow to bury everything, and on the breeze, the barest edge of green apple and moss whispered of possibility.

Epilogue

About One Year Later
Corbin & Alex

ALEX BRUSHED ASIDE Corbin's long hair and kissed the back of his neck. He'd come home to find Corbin asleep at the kitchen table with his head on his crossed arms, and at the press of Alex's lips he came awake slowly.

When he straightened up, Alex kissed his mouth, tasting sleep and ginger and the heat of Corbin's tongue. It was what Alex always did when he got home: kissed Corbin until Corbin's body remembered that this was real. Because sometimes, when they were apart, it folded back in on itself out of habit.

But after a year, the habit was slowly shifting. Now, some mornings Corbin awoke to find his arms had already sought out Alex in sleep, clutching him close. Some evenings after dinner, when they left the house for their nightly walk through the woods, Corbin's hand would reach out automatically, searching for Alex's.

These were the moments Alex held inside himself with quiet satisfaction. The remaking of Corbin Wale was a constant overturning, like the ocean tides.

The remaking of Alex Barrow had been far less tempestuous. It had been a deepening, an underscoring. He had sunk into his love for Corbin with the inevitability of gravity. At unexpected moments, he would see Corbin and be caught breathless at the insistence of his need. When Corbin reached for him, he felt that need like magnets finding their way close enough to snap together.

It was what he'd never had. And now that he did, he could recognize the foolishness of thinking he hadn't wanted it.

They'd made a life that fit them. They'd made their own rules and followed their own whims. And neither of them had ever been happier. For Alex it was a magnification, for Corbin a revelation. But both of them tended it like a fire, feeding it with care, so it warmed and sustained, but didn't consume.

Now, as Corbin came back to him in the kiss, Alex wrapped his arms around him and held him close.

"I made up two new muffin recipes. And I finished the chapter," Corbin said into his neck. Corbin still wasn't much for hellos or pleasantries.

"Yeah? Tell me."

Tell me. They were the magic words. The ones that made Corbin believe his thoughts were welcome, believe his desires and fantasies were cherished, believe his suggestions were valued. *Tell me* had the power to turn him inside out. And Alex kept every secret, every word, safe.

Corbin stretched, shoulders popping from hunching over a counter and a table all day. He'd been up with Alex before the sun. Corbin had come to cherish these predawn hours, when people were still asleep, but nature was stirring. They felt precious and delicate. And Alex's kiss before he left for the bakery felt equally precious, lips lingering as if he could hardly tear himself away.

He still baked in the kitchen of And Son twice a week, but now he preferred to work on recipes from home. He'd turned out to be good at it once he'd allowed his mind to wander in that direction. And he loved the feel of the ingredients in his hands. Loved to watch Alex eat what he'd prepared. Some of his wilder experiments produced inedible results, and Alex tasted them with the same enthusiasm, then teased him with affection and not the slightest hint of rebuke.

"One for summer. I felt so summery this morning," he murmured absently. Alex kissed his jaw. "Sweet cornbread muffin made with browned butter, a few cherries, and a tiny splash of almond extract." He'd daydreamed the sweet summer corn in the garden and the way Alex's lips looked like cherries when swollen with his kisses.

"Mmm, that's a really good idea."

Alex's praise, Alex's *esteem*, undid Corbin like nothing ever had. Well, nothing except Alex's command.

"And, um," Corbin went on, distracted by Alex's mouth at his throat, stubble electrifying his skin. "Gingerbread bran muffin. With molasses and crystallized ginger." He'd daydreamed Alex's constant steady nurturance, studded with moments of spice and snaps of annihilating sweetness.

Alex pulled him closer and hummed. "I could taste it on you. The ginger." He tipped Corbin's chin up and kissed him again, tongues tangling, until Corbin went boneless in his arms.

"You can taste them for real," Corbin whispered, nodding at the counter.

"Muffins for dinner?" Alex said with a last kiss to the corner of Corbin's mouth.

Corbin's sudden smile was shockingly sweet. Sometimes things delighted him that Alex could never predict. And to see Corbin's joy filled Alex with a satisfaction too deep to measure.

"Can we have pancakes too."

"Pancakes too." Alex brushed a kiss over Corbin's mouth and pressed him close, before turning to the refrigerator.

As Alex made the pancakes—Corbin got too distracted and always burned them in the pan—Corbin perched on the counter and told him about the chapter he'd finished.

Corbin was drawing a comic. One morning, a few days after Alex had moved in, Corbin had flipped through his notebooks and felt a pang of loss. He hadn't drawn his friends in weeks. He settled in to reconnect with them, and was startled to realize that it wasn't *them* he missed. It was drawing itself.

He still thought about them often, but he made up stories about them less and less.

Corbin had turned blank pages in his notebook—*three, for luck and distance*—and began to draw. Began to draw something else.

For the first few days, he hadn't been sure of what it was. There were peaked roofs and the tips of pine trees swaying in a green breeze. There were two moons over a rambling garden, and two matching women tending giant pumpkins and cabbages and herbs that scented the air.

And there was a little boy between them, looking out into the woods at the animals he could hear there.

Corbin drew and drew and little by little, the pieces came together.

This boy wasn't lonely because he was loved by all the animals. This boy wasn't afraid because he could fly up toward the moons and look down at the whole of his world and see that it was complete, it was safe. This boy would grow up some day and he would be happy, but slowly, slowly.

Now it had been months and the story had grown larger as his imagination unspooled. They had cleared out the attic, with its mellow wash of light, for him to draw in, and the wooden boards were strewn with drawings, the walls covered in them.

Corbin wasn't sure what he would do with it when he was done. He wasn't sure if he would ever *be* done. But it made him happy, and that was something he'd come to believe was valuable.

After dinner, ginger and cherries and maple syrup still lingering on their tongues, they left the house hand in hand, boots and sweaters and coats pulled on against the snow. When they reached the tree line, a familiar bark rang through the air, and Wolf came to their side. Other dogs barked happily in answer. They'd emerge in time.

The quiet of the air was hypnotizing, and they made their way slowly through the snow.

"Alex."

Alex still felt a thrill every time Corbin said his name. "Yeah, baby."

"It's almost been a year."

Corbin had felt the season approach like a motor running down in his stomach.

"It has. Tell me what you're thinking."

"I don't know what will happen. I . . . If I did it wrong, if the curse didn't break . . ." He shook his head. They both knew what Corbin thought it meant. "I'm scared I'll lose you."

Alex stopped him with a tug to his hand. "You're not going to lose me."

"I might."

"Nope. Not going to happen."

"Alex." Corbin knew that Alex didn't believe in the curse, not exactly. But he believed in the power of people to make things happen, or to succumb to them. He might not worry about the curse itself, but he worried about Corbin's thrall to it.

Alex pulled Corbin in and hugged him, their embrace a bulky thing of coats and hats and scarves. "When will you know? It's *within a year*, right, so when do we measure from? Is it from when I fell in love, or from when you did? Or the first day we both were? God, this is worse than figuring out an anniversary."

Corbin pushed him away, smiling. "You're ridiculous. You know it doesn't work that way."

Alex grinned. He had no idea how it worked, but had some ideas about how Corbin's mind worked. He was smart and creative, and if given an opportunity to make connections, he would.

"Tell me how it works, love."

Corbin shrugged.

"How will you know when we're safe?"

Corbin shrugged again. "I'll just know."

TWO DAYS LATER, Corbin woke gasping in the dark.

His head was spinning and there were spangles in his chest. His fingertips were numb.

"Alex," he croaked.

"Mmm, you okay, baby?" Alex murmured, still half asleep.

"Alex, it's today."

Alex shifted next to him, coming awake at the panic in his voice. "Tell me."

"Alex." Corbin pushed off the covers and made for the window. He searched the skies and the treetops and the snow below for signs. He closed his eyes and felt his own heartbeat and the rush of blood through his body. He felt Alex's heartbeat across the room, as strong and vital as ever.

He stuck his head out the window, taking in great gasps of air, filtering out the earthy smells of winter in search of the ones that could tell him something.

"Alex."

Alex's arms came around him, and Alex's chin came down on top of his head. They were both naked, and Corbin could feel their goose bumps everywhere.

"So we just have to get through today, right? And if we do, you'll believe that we're okay?"

Corbin nodded and let himself be led back to bed. His heart was pounding so hard he felt faint. The span of one day stood between him and everything he'd ever wanted, or something that would destroy him.

"Is it midnight, tonight, or do we have to get through until tomorrow morning? Like, morning to evening, or twenty-four hours, or—"

Corbin socked him in the shoulder.

"Should we stay in bed all day? Will we be safer?"

"Aunt Jade's wife died in her sleep."

"Okay, should we just go about our business as usual?"

"It doesn't matter. If it's going to happen, it will happen."

Corbin shuddered and Alex drew him close, lying down with Corbin on his chest.

"I know, baby. I meant what would make *you* feel better."

But Corbin didn't know.

Alex went to work as usual, promising Corbin he'd text every hour and be home by four. When he kissed Corbin goodbye at the door, Corbin was shaking so badly his teeth chattered. When their lips parted, Corbin whimpered like a distressed animal and Alex could hardly bear to leave him. But Corbin had told him to go, finally, saying it would be harder to watch him all day, waiting.

Alex texted every hour, as promised—more than every hour. He sent Corbin pictures of pies and croissants, scones and cookies. He sent a picture of himself holding up a loaf of bread and said he'd bring it home for dinner. Corbin looked at all of them, running his fingers over the screen of the phone Alex had insisted he get.

It had two contacts in it: Alex and Gareth. Gareth liked to send him text messages consisting entirely of emojis, which Corbin would read the way he read the signs, and respond appropriately.

As he thought of Gareth, a text from him came through. This one was not in emojis.

If Alex dies, I'll still like you. And I won't be mad at you for killing my best friend with your love.

Corbin snorted. Gareth's combination of fierce loyalty and abrasive honesty had become a welcome part of his life over the past year.

If Alex dies I'll probably die too and save you the trouble, Corbin wrote back. He half believed it was true. That Alex's removal from the world would erase him.

You're an idiot, Gareth texted. *Tell me if you want me to come over.*

Too restless to draw anymore, Corbin found himself wandering the house in thick wool socks, a sweater, and sweatpants that Alex had bought him, insisting that while he should still *please* sleep naked, it might be nice for him to have something comfortable to lounge around in. As with most things that Corbin had never considered for himself, Alex had been right.

He paced the hallway, watching dust motes dance and glimmer in the milky sunlight, until finally he pushed open the door to Aunt Hilda's bedroom.

Corbin hadn't opened this door since the day his aunts' bodies were taken away. The room was choked in dust and absence, and as Corbin eased inside, it felt like he was falling through into another time.

The bed where the aunts' bodies had lain was bare, and it drew Corbin's eye like a lodestone. He walked around the perimeter of the room, running a palm along the wall as if he was drawing a circle. When he got to the bed, he reached a hand out like a divining rod, but he felt nothing dark lurking there.

Slowly, as if he were a child, he climbed up on the bare mattress, and curled at the foot of the bed, as he had that day and for the days that followed.

The aunts had loved him in their own way. He knew that now, though he had never considered it when they were alive. They hadn't given him what he needed—he knew that now, too—but they hadn't withheld anything out of malice or stinginess. They simply hadn't known. And ignorance was painful, but it wasn't the same as a lack of love.

They had told him the stories they knew, imparted the beliefs they held dear. They had given him the world as they understood it, and tried their best to arm him for it.

He stayed curled there for what felt like a long while, remembering. Remembering Aunt Hilda's tenderness for her many cats and Aunt Jade's trembly laugh. Aunt Hilda's marshmallow root tea and Aunt Jade's cinnamon toast. Rainy mornings sitting in easy silence and late nights listening to the aunts talk in low voices when they didn't know he could hear.

He missed them sharply all of a sudden, like a fishhook to his gut. He let it wash over him, and then he let it ebb. As he left the room with a lingering touch to the carvings of the phases of the moon around the four-poster bed, Corbin thought he felt the air heave a creaking sigh and let something go.

That night, Alex and Corbin were both too on edge to talk much, so they read on the couch in front of the fire, Corbin leaning on Alex, Dreidel leaning on Corbin. Corbin couldn't concentrate and he lost himself in watching the fire instead, imagining it as a cleansing force, protecting them, burning up all the bad energy and leaving them with only peace. Alex couldn't concentrate much better and soon abandoned his book to run his hands through Corbin's hair, twisting it around his fingers and braiding chunks of it in complex braids like he would challah dough.

They went to bed soon after, early, eager for the day to end.

Corbin was so exhausted from being anxious all day that he didn't have the energy to put his fear into words. He didn't have the energy to look into Alex's eyes and say *I love you. I didn't even know what love was until I loved you. I'm so afraid I might lose you. Please don't let this be the last kiss, the last touch. Hold me all night, please don't let go.*

But it didn't matter, because Alex already knew those things. He knew Corbin's love as he knew his own, and he pulled Corbin to him in the dark, skin against skin, and held on tight, drifting to sleep on Corbin's tempestuous seas.

They woke in a cocoon of warm breath and tangled limbs. Outside, snow had been falling heavily for hours, feet of it, grinding the world to a halt.

It was early morning, the sunlight shining through the falling snow.

Corbin came awake slowly, then jerked upright. He pushed at Alex and pressed a trembling hand to his chest.

"You're alive."

Alex's eyes stayed closed, and he grumbled as he batted Corbin's questing hands away.

"Alex. Alex!"

Alex blinked sleepily. Then he saw Corbin's grin, as pure and bright as a beam of sunlight.

"I'm alive."

"You're alive. Alex."

Corbin's smile trembled, and then he burst into tears, great wracking sobs that shook his shoulders.

Alex smiled. Corbin's emotions were so close to the surface that sometimes they overflowed. Alex was honored that he was allowed to witness it.

He wrapped Corbin in his arms and pushed him down to the bed, then he lay on top of him. It was the way Corbin felt safest—held down, enveloped, overwhelmed. He smiled as Corbin scrabbled at his back and finally got his arms around him where he wanted them. He smiled as Corbin's sobs turned to soft snuffles and then the occasional shuddering breath. He smiled as Corbin went boneless beneath him.

He smiled because, though he hadn't known when the day would come that Corbin would trust in this completely, he'd been waiting for it. Now that it was here, he felt as light as the falling snow.

Corbin was whispering nonsense into his neck, and Alex pressed his stubbled cheek against Corbin's smooth one.

"I love you," he said into Corbin's ear. "I will always love you." And Corbin shuddered beneath him. "I love you," he said again, and felt Corbin's relief spark into arousal. It happened for him sometimes—the strength of one feeling transmuting almost instantly into another.

Alex ran warm palms over Corbin's body beneath the covers, stroking his chest and stomach, his arms and fingers, his hips and thighs. Corbin never opened his eyes, just kept whispering nonsense and whimpering as the spark between them burned hotter and hotter.

"AlexAlexAlexAlexAlex" poured from his lips, and they came together effortlessly, Alex sliding inside Corbin and feeling like he had finally come home. Corbin's potent imagination often turned sex into something transcendent and magical, and Alex treasured those times.

Now, though, it felt like Corbin was *there* with him, so present he was like a shard of glass. They locked eyes, and Alex moved them with his thrusts, powerful and insistent. He rocked inside Corbin and the pleasure washed over him. Corbin threw his head back and cried out. They grabbed at each other, fingers digging in, hips thrusting, mouths meeting and tongues tangling, until they were one body—blood and bone and sweat and come, surging together like a tidal wave.

Corbin whimpered as he came, his limbs seizing up, his body quaking, and then going boneless, and Alex's orgasm burned up the base of his spine and then exploded as he drove himself deep inside.

It was what Corbin always wanted—what Alex always wanted to give him. To be taken over entirely by Alex, every empty space filled up. To feel Alex inside him everywhere and forever.

After, they kissed lazily, hands finding each other. Then they drifted, as the snow fell outside, hearts beating in rhythm, arms and legs braiding together as morning turned to day, day turned into night, and night gathered itself toward another morning. Another, and another, and another.

THE END

DEAR READER,

Thank you so much for reading *The Remaking of Corbin Wale*! I hope you enjoyed Corbin and Alex's story.

If you did, consider spreading the word! You can help others find this book by writing reviews, blogging about it, and talking about it on social media. Reviews and shares really help authors keep writing, and we appreciate them so much! The power is in your hands.

Thank you!

xo, Roan Parrish

Want to get exclusive content and news of future book releases? Sign up for my **newsletter** on **roanparrish.com**!

Acknowledgments

10% of the proceeds of this book go to the Russian LGBT Network. I'm grateful that my words might go some small distance to materially impacting things in a positive way.

A huge thanks to my early readers, who approached this project with such generosity. Your excitement, questions, and suggestions were instrumental.

To my agent, Courtney Miller-Callihan, who, when I texted her, *What if I were doing something kind of bonkers*, and described it, merely replied, *That sounds insane and potentially amazing*. Thank you for always being willing to see the amazing side.

Thanks to everyone who's made Chanukah magical for me over the years. I hope I returned the favor, just a little.

Last and most, to my sister, who knows why. You're the fire.

About the Author

Roan Parrish lives in Philadelphia where she is gradually attempting to write love stories in every genre.

When not writing, she can usually be found cutting her friends' hair, meandering through whatever city she's in while listening to torch songs and melodic death metal, or cooking overly elaborate meals. She loves bonfires, winter beaches, minor chord harmonies, and self-tattooing. One time she may or may not have baked a six-layer chocolate cake and then thrown it out the window in a fit of pique.

MORE INFORMATION

Keep up with all my new releases and get exclusive free content by signing up for my **NEWSLETTER** at **roanparrish.com**.

Come join **PARRISH OR PERISH**, my Facebook group, to hang out, chat about books, and get exclusive news, updates, excerpts of works in progress, freebies, and pictures of my cat!

You can follow me on **BOOKBUB** and **AMAZON** to find out when my books are on sale.

You can follow me on **PINTEREST** at ARoanParrish, to see visuals of all my characters, books, and settings. And you can follow me on **TWITTER**, **FACEBOOK**, and **INSTAGRAM** at RoanParrish.

Also by Roan Parrish

The Middle of Somewhere Series:

In the Middle of Somewhere

Out of Nowhere

Where We Left Off

The Small Change Series:

Small Change

Invitation to the Blues

The Remaking of Corbin Wale

Heart of the Steal (with Avon Gale)

Short fiction:

Mayfair (in *Lead Me Into Darkness: Five Halloween Tales of Paranormal Romance*)

Company (in *All In Fear: A Collection of Six Horror Tales*)

CPSIA information can be obtained
at www.ICGtesting.com
Printed in the USA
LVHW020817271021
701667LV00004BA/555

9 780998 967172